END MATTERS

Chinazom Akobundu Godwin

End Matters

© **Chinazom Akobundu Godwin, 2020**

ISBN: 978-978-988-687-6

Published by Ugochinazom Productions Limited

Book cover designed by Hoopla Hive

Author's Contact

Email: chinazomagu@yahoo.com, akosconunique@gmail.com

For

Engr. Kelechi Nnabuihe Godwin and Mrs Chiamaka Adachukwu Godwin,

You put in a lot of effort like my parents for me to become who I am today.

Thanks a million!

CONTENTS

CHAPTER ONE

The sky was aglow with the evening sun, and the gentle breeze caressed Ejiofor Isiawele's exposed skin. His arrival at Senator Ekwueme's mansion was a fateful occasion. As soon as the gates opened, he could not help but admire the beautiful sight before him. He sauntered down to the main building with leisurely composure. A red Bentley Continental GT stood out in the garage with other exotic cars.

Ejiofor knew his brother, Senator Ekwueme, to be a very wealthy politician, but he had no idea he had completed one of the most beautiful houses in Maitama just within a year of his being away from Nigeria. He had taken the time to explore the streets while in the car that his brother had sent to the airport to pick him. Ejiofor had been to Ekwueme's other houses, but it was the first time he would step into the new Abuja residence.

His mind drifted back to their childhood days. He had always known his elder brother to be a hardworking person, but he never imagined that he would amass such wealth at such a young age, let alone be the Senate President of Nigeria.

He shrugged. He was finally starting to believe what people said about hard work and determination being the ultimate keys to success. *'Check the meaning of determination in the dictionary and you would most likely find Ekwueme's picture next to it.'* He thought.

"I am really happy for him. A win for him is a win for the whole family," Ejiofor murmured as his eyes scanned the large compound, decorated in great taste with flowerpots. His eyes shifted to the main building, "Whoever painted this must be an expert," he praised aloud.

He always knew that his elder brother had an affinity for white paints, and it did not surprise him to realize that every one of his houses was painted in the same colour white. Ejiofor admired the compound with all its grandeur.

For a moment, he dreamt of having a similar home for relaxation purposes when he was older and made. He was still admiring the compound and soliloquizing when a slim, tall man emerged from the mansion and walked up to him.

"Good day, Mr Ejiofor. Senator Ekwueme is waiting for you in the living room."

Ejiofor nodded and followed him into the mansion. He could not help but throw occasional glances at the magnificent interior of the house.

Wow! This is beautiful.' Ejiofor thought. *'There are levels to this kind of wealth.*' He walked in and met his elder brother, Ekwueme. "Good evening, sir," he greeted.

A long time ago, he had learnt to address his elder brother in this way as a sign of respect.

"Ejims, Nwannem." Ekwueme wrapped his arms around Ejiofor in a tight hug. "How was your flight?"

"It was great. Thank you, sir." Ejiofor grinned.

"How are mother and father doing?" Ekwueme inquired.

"They are fine," he answered, sitting majestically on one of the gold-coloured armchairs beside Ekwueme. "They sent their greetings." Ejiofor cleared his throat. "The life of a senator has refined your complexion. With your cherry red lips and pointed nose, you look like an Indian and a Briton in one body."

Ekwueme burst into laughter. They talked and laughed over whatever past comic incident they could think of when a dark-skinned lady, with well-endowed hip, hobbled into the living room. Ejiofor's eyes were fixed on the television and he barely paid attention to her. The only time he raised his head to acknowledge her presence was when his brother addressed the lady as 'darling', indicating endearment.

The horrified look on Ejiofor's face was obvious as his eyes met with the lady's. Ekwueme's eyes moved from his brother and settled on the lady who was too busy staring at Ejiofor to notice Ekwueme's eyes were on her.

"Ebony?" Ejiofor finally spoke.

"Ejiofor," the lady who had an equally apprehensive look on her face called out to Ejiofor in a shaky tone.

Ejiofor could tell that her heartbeat and discomfort had tripled. It was one of those moments where he witnessed an opponent wishing the ground would open and swallow him or her.

He turned to his elder brother briefly and noticed how he looked at Ebony with curious eyes. No doubt, Ekwueme was wondering how his wife-to-be and his kid brother knew each other. If only Ekwueme had not rushed the introduction. If only he had brought the girl of his choice home right from day one. If only his brother had introduced his lady, this mistake of a person would not be anywhere near this beautiful mansion.

Ekwueme cleared his throat after the 'staring contest' lingered for too long. Ejiofor blinked and looked away, ignoring his brother's sigh of relief. He stared ahead with anger written all over his face.

Ebony lowered her head and fumbled with her fingers. Ejiofor was sure she was only trying to hide her discomfort.

The previous weekend, his mother had called to tell him that his brother went for an impromptu introduction at his lady's place, and plans were underway for them to get married. They were going to have their traditional and church wedding on the same day.

He was excited about the news of his brother's marriage until his mother mentioned the name 'Ebony'. Although, the name had taken him aback, he would have waved it off as a coincidence, but his mother had mentioned that the girl was also from Bhasekoh local government in Leari State.

He did not want to scare his mother by asking too many questions, so he had taken it upon himself to carry out investigations before the marriage.

This was the sole purpose of his visit to his brother's house, and now that the evidence was staring right at him, he was short of words. It never occurred to him that his brother would be interested in a lady like Ebony, and go as far as marrying her. Did he really know her? Or was he just blind to the truth about her?

Ekwueme broke the stinging silence enveloping the room. "I see you both know each other, so there is no need for an introduction." He smiled. "Darling, my brother will be spending some time with us."

"How many days is he staying?" Ebony asked without hesitation.

Ejiofor's eyes widened in disgust. He would have answered the question, but for the respect, he had for his elder brother.

"He will stay for as long as he wants," Ekwueme answered dismissively.

Ejiofor looked back at Ebony, and as expected, she had eyes running from one part of the living room to another, except his direction.

He was satisfied with her reaction, and he was more than willing to keep evoking such reactions until she stopped whatever game she was up to with his brother.

Ejiofor spied on Ekwueme briefly. His brother was such a wonderful and generous person. In fact, he possessed every character necessary to qualify as a 'perfect' man, but with this person in his life, Ejiofor was sure of an inevitable change and he was not about to allow that, not on his watch. The lady was not fit for his brother, and he would stop at nothing until he had opened his brother's eyes to the truth.

CHAPTER TWO

Ebony's thoughts were in disarray. She wondered why Ejiofor had decided to show up, as she could not get rid of the anxiety his cold reception brought. The way Ejiofor stared at her with contempt written all over his face, smote her. She had to admit she had done some wrong things in the past, but she was only human.

"Darling," Ekwueme called to her. "You should tell Adanne what to cook so Ejiofor can eat and have some rest."

Ten seconds passed, and there was neither a response from Ebony nor a sign of movement. She shuddered when Ekwueme called her again. This time his voice raised a notch higher, enough to take her out of her reverie.

"What did you say?" Ebony asked.

"Please, ask Adanne to prepare something for Ejiofor to eat."

Ebony tried to hide her frown. She did not want to step out of the living room because she knew that Ejiofor would spill everything about her past to Ekwueme, and that was the last thing she wanted in this lifetime. Everything in her life was starting to normalize and go the way she had always dreamed, but with Ejiofor's presence and his countenance, she was not so sure anymore.

Right from the moment she set eyes on him, she had tried to think of something to do to save her face and reputation, but his hard and mischievous stare made her brain go blank. Ejiofor did not make any attempt to mask his hatred towards her, and she was sure beyond measure that even if she pleaded with him to keep her secret, he would never agree to it.

Seeing that Ebony was not ready to do as she was told, Ekwueme turned to Ejiofor. "Maybe you should take your bags inside and take a shower," he suggested. "I'm sure you will have something to eat by the time you come out."

As they got off the couch and started towards the passage, Ebony looked from one brother to the other. Ekwueme wore a neutral expression, while Ejiofor still had his angry 'what-is-she-doing-here' kind of expression. Ebony wished he would give her a chance to talk with him and straighten things out.

"The second room to the left should be perfect for you. I had someone fix it before you came in." Ekwueme informed Ejiofor.

Ejiofor muttered, "Thank you." to his brother with a half-smile on his lips.

Ebony could tell that the smile was feigned. She tried not to dwell on that because his smile did not matter to her. What she wanted was a way out, or a plan to make him keep his mouth shut.

She avoided Ejiofor's gaze and turned to Ekwueme. "Darling, please can I talk to you?"

Ekwueme stared at her for a while before he shrugged. "Give me a minute," he said to Ejiofor.

They walked into one of the spare rooms close by, and Ebony turned to Ekwueme, staring at him inquisitively. "You didn't mention that your brother was coming."

"Darling, I'm really sorry. I forgot."

"You should have at least said something earlier," Ebony went on. "You know I'm not too good with surprises."

Ekwueme gently took her right hand. "I'm truly sorry. His request to visit also surprised me. Ejiofor is not much of a traveller. I could not decline his request or even hesitate, so he would not feel like I did not want him or something. Remember, he was not at the introduction. I felt it is right for him to meet my wife."

"We already know each other." Ebony pointed out.

"I know," Ekwueme replied. "But he's meeting my wife, not just Ebony."

Ebony's heart skipped at his first statement. *'Did he already find out my secret? No way!'* She wondered.

She dismissed the thoughts. If he already knew the secret, she would not be standing in his house, and Ejiofor would not be staring at her in that manner.

"How did you know?" She asked.

He yawned. "I noticed the way you two looked at each other. So how did you know my brother?"

This question startled Ebony for a split second. She had not expected that he would ask so soon.

"I knew him back at Bhasekoh, but it was a long time ago," Ebony answered with a shaky edge to her tone that Ekwueme did not seem to notice. "I will personally prepare something for him to eat, just to welcome him, but," her eyes pleaded, "next time, please let me know when someone is coming over. I don't want to be perceived as an incompetent fiancée."

"Wife," Ekwueme countered, with a smile.

Ebony felt her heart swell with joy. She truly liked the sound of that, and she could not wait to make it official. Countless times, she had tried her wedding gown in her room. She imagined herself dressed in a sparkling white gown, a beautiful tiara gracing her head, and her hands firmly gripping a bouquet, while walking down the aisle to meet the love of her life, Ekwueme-the only man who captured her heart at first sight.

They walked back hand in hand into the passage where Ejiofor was waiting with the same angry facial expression.

Once again, Ebony's state of unrest came back to mind. "Let me show you to your room," Ebony volunteered, looking over Ejiofor's head.

"I'm fine," Ejiofor replied in a cold tone. "I will find it myself."

Ebony kept mute. Her instincts told her that he was going to decline, but she had hoped he would let her, so they could talk. She became apprehensive when a thought occurred to her. Clearly, he was not here to talk things out but to embarrass her.

As Ejiofor headed in the direction Ekwueme had described in hurried steps, Ekwueme turned towards the living room but decided to go with him. Ebony, who was fidgeting at this point, knew there was nothing she could do except to tag along with the brothers.

To make Ekwueme slow down, she thought of a question. "What about the Deputy Senate President's visit?"

Ekwueme stopped briefly and turned to face her. "They should be here any moment from now."

Ebony seized the opportunity to take his hand. "I can't wait to have him in our home," she said, purposely making him slow down his steps.

When they finally got to Ejiofor's room, he had locked the door. Ekwueme knocked a few times, but there was no response.

Ekwueme shook his head in resignation. "He's probably in the shower. I will go and take care of something else." He looked straight into Ebony's eyes. "Please, go ahead and start preparing the meal. I sincerely appreciate your help."

She nodded with a smile and left for the kitchen while Ekwueme went back to the living room.

In the kitchen, Ebony had satisfaction written all over her face. She had foiled the first attempt by Ejiofor to embarrass her.

She knew Ejiofor did not open the door because she was with Ekwueme, and that alone gave her joy because that was the goal. She had intentionally talked aloud as soon as they neared the door, just to announce her presence.

Ebony chuckled. She was determined to keep preventing all of Ejiofor's effort to talk to his brother alone. There was no way Ejiofor would reveal her secret to his brother. "It's not over until I say it is over." She smirked.

CHAPTER THREE

Ekwueme sat in the living room when the doorbell blared. A domestic staff went to answer it and ran back in.

"Sir," he bowed.

Ekwueme looked up from his laptop. "Yes, Ayo?"

"The Deputy Senate President and some other people are here to see you."

Ekwueme nodded. "Let them in. I have been expecting them."

Ayo nodded affirmatively and did as he was instructed.

The Deputy Senate President, Senator Adams, Senator Ayomide, Senator Takwas, and Senator Ezeuwa, who seemed to be in their early forties, walked into Senator Ekwueme's living room. They all had sincere smiles spread across their faces. Obviously, they had good reasons for showing up in Senator Ekwueme's home.

Ekwueme stood to exchange pleasantries with them. "Senator Adam's!" he bellowed to his deputy. "Welcome, welcome, welcome! How have you been?"

Senator Adams was taller and dark with tribal marks on his cheeks. Adams stretched his hand for a handshake. "I've been good and gearing up. I can't wait to start serving the good people of this country."

The men burst into laughter. They had just been elected and were yet to officially start their duties in the National House of Assembly.

11

"I look forward to that as well," Ekwueme concurred.

The other senators took their turn in shaking Ekwueme's hand amidst exuberant chatting. Ekwueme looked in the direction of the kitchen. He would have loved for Ebony to come to greet his guests, so he could introduce her as his wife-to-be. However, he understood she was busy, as Ejiofor could be hungry. He decided it was best to let her finish cooking, as the introduction could hold on a bit.

Adanne, a domestic staff, served drinks and the men had their glass cups in their hands, talking and laughing excitedly.

"I was talking to Senator Ezeuwa about the proposed wardrobe allowances, and our thoughts don't seem to align," Senator Adams said. "But that is by the way. Where is your fiancée?"

"She's in the kitchen. My younger brother just arrived from Leari, so she is making something for him to eat."

Ekwueme noticed the shock on the other senators' face when the words came out of his mouth.

"She will surely make a homely wife," Ayomide said, with a smile.

"She cooks?" Adams whispered. "The wife-to-be of a Senate President of the Federal Republic of Nigeria cooks in the kitchen?"

Ekwueme laughed heartily. He saw that coming. "She's a great cook. She volunteered to do this just to welcome my younger brother. She likes to cook too." The genuine surprise on their faces brought him joy. He knew that his wife's cooking was the last thing they expected to hear when they walked into his home.

"You got yourself a rare gem." Senator Takwas complimented.

"I sure did," Ekwueme's smile deepened. "I am amazed that women like her still exist on this planet. She's beautiful, she's generous, she respects everyone, and above all, she is the lady with the key to my heart."

Ekwueme meant every word he said. He had met other ladies in the past and he knew from day one, he could not start a courtship with them, let alone marry them. He was a man of principles and he was not interested in marrying a woman who had no principle or dignity.

Meeting Ebony was a miracle, and he did not regret waiting for someone as amazing as her in his life. She had been everything he wanted in a woman, and more. The moment they crossed paths, marrying her became the only thing on his mind. With her, he knew he would always be a happy man.

With the smile on the faces of the other senators, it was obvious that they were happy for him. Ekwueme wished that they had attended his introduction ceremony, so they could see Ebony looking radiant with her signature smile gracing her beautiful face. Nonetheless, they still had the wedding to attend.

While he was thinking about her, Ebony majestically walked into the living room, smiling. "Good evening, sirs." She bobbed. "You are all welcome."

"Good evening," they answered in unison.

Senator Adams turned to Ekwueme with an arched eyebrow and widened eyes. Ekwueme nodded in response, and Adams slightly opened his mouth to express his surprise.

Senator Ekwueme stretched his hand to Ebony. She took it, walked towards him, and sat with him.

"Senators," Ekwueme addressed the men, and they all focused their attention on him. "Meet my fiancée. Her name is Ebony. She is the woman after my own heart."

"She's truly stunning," Senator Adams noted.

"Thank you," Ebony answered.

Ekwueme beamed with pride. Even if he was not sure he had made the right choice, now he knew from the assertive look and gleam of pride on the faces of the other senators.

"They came to get the wedding card," Ekwueme informed Ebony.

"We need to make the public announcement," Senator Adams chipped in.

"Okay. That's great." She nodded. "Let me get some cards. Please, excuse me."

Ebony left to get the cards from the room. The men kept chatting and showering praises on Ekwueme, on how he had taken one of the best women in town for keeps.

"You went to market with your eyes open," Senator Adams grinned.

"He even wore a double-lens pair of glasses," Senator Ezeuwa chuckled.

They were still talking when Ebony emerged with the exquisite and tastefully patterned gold-coloured wedding cards.

She handed them over to Senator Ekwueme. "I brought five."

"That should be enough," he answered, taking the cards from her. "Thank you."

Ekwueme handed the cards to the senators, and while they complimented the cards, Ebony informed Ekwueme that she would like to go back to the kitchen.

Ekwueme urged her to go. "Ejiofor must be hungry now," he stated. "Get someone to assist you, so you don't overstress yourself."

"I'm good," Ebony answered. A tight-lipped smile followed, and she turned to the other senators, "I will be right back, sirs. Once again, I appreciate the compliments and kind words."

Senator Adams was the first to speak up. "You are welcome, Ebony. We will be seeing more of each other soon, and again, you are my boss's wife, please call me Adams. Drop the 'sir' thing, I'm not even old yet."

"All right, Mr Adams." She smiled at the other senators, curtsied, and gracefully walked back to the kitchen.

"I'm still shocked," Adams said. "You picked the best. She's so beautiful and nice."

"I told you," Ekwueme said with pride.

"Does she have a younger sister," Adams asked.

Senator Ekwueme rolled his eyes at him. "Don't go there."

"Oh, so you think you're the only one who likes a good woman?" Adams grinned.

"You have married one already. That one is enough for you," Senator Ezeuwa chipped in.

They all laughed.

"I wish you the very best, my President," Ayomide said.

"Thank you. It's God. I asked for a wife, and He gave me the best."

CHAPTER FOUR

All compliments from the senators were etched on Ebony's memory, and she intended for it to remain that way with wishes for more encomiums. But that was not to be.

If anyone ever told her Ejiofor could show up in her life again, she would have laughed at such a person. Unfortunately, he did show up as her worst nightmare. She knew this because of his judgemental expressions. He looked determined to get back at her. He looked ready to throw her belongings out of his brother's house.

Ebony had a little secret of her own though, and Ejiofor's presence would no longer be a burden to her. She was already making plans to take care of that. The corners of her lips twitched in amusement.

She had sneaked to Ejiofor's room after leaving the senators and knocked at the door. She begged to have a word with him. But since he did not want to talk, she was ready to play the game his way. Just actions, no more talks!

She picked up the small bowl of vegetable soup that she had left to defrost and poured its content into a medium-sized pot. The smile on her face was evidence that she was truly pleased with herself, and her plans to deal with Ejiofor.

After placing the pot on a burner, she stepped behind the kitchen door and smiled when she spotted a flower among the set of flowerpots that decorated the little space. She had noticed it during her second visit to Ekwueme's house.

She quickly bent over and cut some of the flower. She weighed the portion of flower in her hand and gave a satisfied smile that it was enough to do the trick without suspicion. She walked back in, washed it, and cut it into thin slices.

She smiled like a wild evil cat and dumped the flower into the pot containing the defrosted vegetable soup, just as Adanne, a domestic staff, walked into the kitchen and offered to assist.

"Go do some other work."

Ebony declined. "I can take care of this myself."

"But, ma'am..."

"I said you should leave; don't you have ears?" Ebony yelled.

Adanne curtsied and scampered out of the kitchen.

Ebony stared at the pot. *'Ejiofor, you didn't give me a choice.'* She thought. If only he had allowed her to explain, then he would know that she had no evil intentions towards Ekwueme. She loved him from the depth of her heart, and she did not think she would be able to survive it if Ejiofor said something to make Senator Ekwueme discard the idea of marrying her.

Ebony soon started to heat the soup, stirring it so the flowers would blend thoroughly with the rest of the soup. Satisfied with her work, she covered the pot and sauntered to the sink. She carefully washed everything that the flowers had encountered, including the knife, and chopping board. A few minutes later, the soup was well heated and ready to serve.

She was about bringing down the pot from the gas cooker when she heard footsteps from behind. Ebony shivered and almost dropped the pot.

With shaky hands, she turned to see who was behind her. Lo and behold, it was Ejiofor. He stared at her like one would stare at one's ruthless enemy. Ebony's heart raced faster than it had ever done since he walked into the house.

She was scared to her bones. Had he seen her? Was he suspicious? Did he know about her plans?

Ejiofor hissed loudly and walked past her to the sink. He washed his hands in the sink and turned to go without sparing her a glance.

With the numerous questions begging for answers in her mind, Ebony felt like her legs would give way if she tried to stand for another minute. She walked back and leaned on the counter.

"Ejiofor," she called. "Let's talk, please."

He turned to her with a mischievous look on his face. "Does it look like I want to talk to you? You have no shame, do you?"

"Ejiofor, I mean no harm whatsoever. I love your brother."

"Tell me a better joke." The tone of his voice was harsh, and Ebony recoiled in fear.

"I know you don't believe me," Ebony said. She was surprised she could still talk given his angry expression and tone. "But that's the truth. I love your brother, and I mean no harm. He's a good person, and I can't take undue advantage of that."

"Ebony, can you even hear yourself?" He asked, mimicked her words, and rolled his eyes at her.

"Let's settle this without involving your brother, please."

"What I want is simple. Pack your bags, call off the wedding, and get the hell out of my brother's life, and house."

Ebony sighed. He was asking for the impossible. How could she just abandon the kind of life she had always wanted when she was just starting to enjoy it? That would be like giving a pack of candy to a hungry child, then asking the child to look at the pack and return it. *'That is wickedness at its peak.'*

"Ejiofor, we all have a past," Ebony reminded him.

"Sure," he answered. "This is why you should always think about the future because you are not going to remain in the past or present forever. If you had an iota of sense and conscience left in you, you would be packing your things to leave my brother's house."

"I can't do..."

Ejiofor wagged his finger at her with a smirk. "Hope you are not thinking I will allow my brother to marry you?"

Ebony's fears changed into something more dangerous than fear. Tears started to streak down her cheeks. She clapped her hands in a plea. The wicked smile on his face told her the plea would be the same as pouring water into a basket.

"Ebony, you are smart, but I will outsmart your smartness. I didn't spend all those years in school for nothing. You can play my brother because he is kind, and 'in love', but you cannot play me."

His blunt words scared Ebony. "I've changed," she stuttered.

"Miss Leopard can you change your spots?" He cocked an eyebrow. "Changing does not automatically mean you've become good for my brother."

"I have. I can swear to you, Ejiofor. Don't do this to me, please."

He hissed and mimicked her again. "Keep your swearing to yourself but rest assured that you are not marrying my brother. Not on my watch. I will make sure he sees the real you before I leave this house. After everything you've done, you want to start parading yourself as a good wife material. Trust me, you will leave this house before me, that I can guarantee you." He said with a note of finality, and without another glance in Ebony's direction, he hurried out of the kitchen.

Ebony exhaled deeply. "Ejiofor, I truly wish you had listened to me," she marched back to the pot and picked it with shaky hands. "Now, you leave me no choice!"

She grabbed plates from the rack and started to dish the soup. Earlier on, when the soup was defrosting, she had made semolina to go with it. She wrapped the semolina in nylons.

She yanked out a tray on which she arranged the soup and wraps of semolina. She headed to the dining table with hope that her plan succeeds. She called out to Adanne and asked her to inform Ejiofor that his food was ready. With her heart still beating hard against her chest, she walked back to clear the kitchen.

CHAPTER FIVE

In a blaze of fury, Ejiofor punched some furniture in his room. It was a large room with a king-sized bed, an armchair, and some nice paintings hanging on the wall. Ejiofor was yet to relish the luxury of the tastefully furnished house because Ebony's presence in the house irritated him to his bones.

Ejiofor scoffed and shook his head. "She had the effrontery to talk to me in that way!"

When Ejiofor first saw her and confirmed his worst fears, he actually thought Ebony was going to get scared and start confessing all her sins, but no, she was still in the house, acting like a good wife material and a perfect woman.

If not for self-restraint, he wished to go back to the kitchen, grab her by the neck with his bare hands and hurl her out of his brother's house and life.

Ebony had foiled his first attempt to speak to his brother about the kind of girl he had in his house. He had to give it to her for winning the first round. She was cunning, but he was smart—way smarter than she ever imagined.

Ejiofor's mind drifted back to all the times he made sacrifices for Ebony in the past. The times he had to literally take a bullet for her. The times he was mocked because of her. Since he saw her, he had tried not to think about the past, but he could not help it any longer. She was an ingrate, and he would never forgive her for that. There was no way in the world he would allow his brother to get married to such a lady. The introduction was a mistake, and he would not sit and allow the worst mistake to happen.

"If she thinks she can marry my brother and start reaping what she did not sow then she must be deluded," he said softly.

Ejiofor recalled the voices he had heard while going to join his brother in the living room. He had paused to know if he would recognize the voices of the visitors but he could not. The only thing he overheard was the praises the visitors showered on Ebony.

Ejiofor walked to the bed and sat on it, but his thoughts kept wandering. There was so much anger in him against Ebony, and all he could think about was how to get his brother to call off the wedding.

He had already forgotten about her, but being the 'leech' that she is, she had wormed her way into his brother's life. The words she had spoken in the kitchen had nauseated him. He rolled his eyes. "A better person my foot!"

He was still brooding and soliloquizing when someone knocked on the door. *'It had better not be Ebony. She's asking for trouble if she's the one knocking on my door again.'*

"Who's there?" He yelled.

"It's me, Adanne," a tender voice said. "Madam said I should tell you that your food is ready."

The knock sounded again.

"Tell your madam that I am not hungry." He answered angrily.

He heard the retreating footsteps and sighed in relief. "Madam," he murmured. "Madam my foot."

He stood and walked to the window. He could not help but wonder how his brother's path crossed with that of a woman like Ebony. There are many good women in the world, why Ebony? Why?

Ejiofor could clearly remember all the times that the family had gathered to talk to Ekwueme about settling down, and in each of those times, he had clearly made it known to them that he was not ready. Then out of the blues, he received the news that his brother was going to seek the hand of a lady in marriage. It happened like something he usually saw in Nollywood movies.

Now that he was thinking about it, he could not help but wonder if his brother was making those decisions by himself or if he was under the influence of some sort of fetish powers. *'Ebony sure seems like she is capable of that, and her level of confidence baffles me.'* He thought.

Wait a minute! He realized he totally missed something. If his mother was friends with Ebony's mother, then something was fishy. His mother had a hand in it. He tried to breathe as the realization hit him.

Even though the family knew that Ekwueme was under pressure to marry due to his new position, their mother probably thought Ekwueme was becoming too old to still be a bachelor. He heaved silently. His mother must be behind the whole arrangement, and Ebony probably used some of those fetish stuff girls like her use to hoodwink rich men.

He heard a knock on his door again. He stared at the door in anger.

"What do you want again?" He bellowed.

"Oga said I should call you."

He shrugged. "Finally, someone of worth is calling me." He smiled but still wondered why Ekwueme had called him. "It had better not be about that girl's food, because I'm not eating." He left the room and strolled into the living room.

At the sight of him, Ekwueme smiled and introduced him to the other senators. "Meet my younger brother, Ejiofor," Ekwueme said, with a hint of pride in his voice. "He was just appointed a Deputy Governor at the Central Bank, so he was sent to London School of Business for one-year training. He just returned two weeks ago. My plan was for him to follow in my footsteps, but he joined Central Bank."

"Wow! Soon, your picture or signature will be on the nation's currency," Senator Ezeuwa said, half-joking. The other senators laughed.

Ejiofor's eyes widened. Obviously, Ekwueme had never discussed such with him, and it surprised and gladdened his heart to hear that his brother had such plans in place for him. They all exchanged pleasantries and Ejiofor left the living room with a smile on his lips.

Halfway to his room, he heard Ebony call his name. "What?" he answered. "I'm getting tired of hearing you call my name."

"Just come and eat," Ebony said in the soberest tone he had ever heard. "If you want me to leave your brother's house, that's fine, but just eat your food."

Ejiofor hissed loudly. "I don't want to eat your food. I have been surviving without you feeding me."

She walked closer and stood beside him. "I'm not trying to feed you. It's your brother's money."

He turned to look at her for the first time. What he saw was not the kind of sight he had imagined. There were tears in her eyes.

Her helplessness amazed Ejiofor. He wondered how she suddenly repented and became so emotional. He frowned. He was not the least bit moved by her tears. A long time ago, he had learnt not to trust women like her. They were capable of doing anything to make people pity them.

"It's my brother's food," he answered. "And my brother's house. You shouldn't be here. Don't think I will fall for these crocodile tears of yours."

He made to walk away, but she held his hands to stop him. He quickly snatched his hands from her with a stern look.

"Keep your hands to yourself," he warned. "Don't ever touch me with those filthy hands."

Ebony lowered her head as tears streaked down her cheeks. "Just eat your food, please. Even if you hate me, you shouldn't starve yourself. Eat! I have nothing against you. It's your brother's food and money. I have set the table for you. I will leave, but I still wish you would just believe that I have changed."

Ejiofor maintained the frown on his face. He could not deny the fact that she was right about one thing—the money and the house belonged to his brother, including the food that she prepared. But, he had already made up his mind to avoid everything that had to do with her, including the food she cooked and whatever part of the house she occupied.

He tried to play stubborn and walk away, but his stomach rumbled in protest. On second thoughts, he walked past her to the dining area and sat.

He would eat the food because it was his brother's money, and he was entitled to it. Before taking his seat at the dining table, he uncovered the plate of soup and inhaled the nice aroma of vegetable soup. He heard footsteps from behind. And when he turned around, he spotted Ebony standing some distance from him.

Ejiofor frowned. First, she begged him to eat. Now, she wanted to watch him eat. Was she up to something? "Would you like to taste from this delicious meal you served me?" He asked.

"Oh, no, don't worry. I'm not hungry," Ebony replied, panting.

"But you're here watching me. So, you either taste from this food, or I won't eat it. This is my final decision."

CHAPTER SIX

Ekwueme was with the senators when he heard murmurs from the dining room. He did not need anyone to tell him Ejiofor and Ebony were at it, even though he could not quite comprehend what the fuss was about.

Paying closer attention, he started to make out some words from their argument; they were talking about food. But what happened to the food? Did Ebony make a mistake or what? From what he knew, Ebony was an amazing cook. So, what was the argument about?

For an instant, he wished he were still in the sitting room with the senators as they were now in a part of the house, he designated as visitors' area—basically a place where he entertained visitors, right next to the living room. Evidence of that were the bottles of wine and glass cups sitting on the mini tables. He made a mental note to ask Ebony and Ejiofor some questions. Their attitudes were confusing. He shook his head and concentrated on his guests.

"I'm more concerned about passing a bill which can give the female child access to her father's inheritance," Ayomide was saying. "I have two daughters, and I am concerned about them and how the world sees them."

"As for me," Senator Ekwueme replied. "Girl or boy, I will try to love my kids equally and appreciate my wife either way. I have witnessed the emotional and physical torture some women go through just because they are unable to bear a male child even when they have four or five girls. It's not what I want to put someone's daughter through."

"You are right," Ayomide responded. "My wife's first role is companionship before we talk about procreation, and whatever gender we end up with at the end of the day is fine by me."

"You both should stop getting emotional over that. The world is changing, more women are starting to stand up for their fundamental human rights," Senator Adams said, waving his hand at both. "My primary concern is education and the falling standard of education. In a country where the phrase 'School Na Scam' is starting to become the order of the day, I'm afraid we won't have many kids bothering about school in the next six or seven years."

"Everybody wants to hustle," Takwas joked, bursting into laughter. "To a large extent, I don't blame them. The internet is wild and misleading. Imagine being in school and seeing your agemate who does not know how to spell his name, driving the latest car in town, flaunting the latest phones and you know, with supposedly 'high-class chicks' by his side. If you were in their shoes, you'd question the essence of schooling and certificates when most of the certificate holders are roaming the streets in search of a job. I think this country needs total rehabilitation."

Ekwueme shook his head. "You are right about that. I sometimes see those things and it makes me wonder if those kids, I mean the ones that flaunt ill-gotten wealth and property, think they will remain young forever. Ill-gotten wealth is only temporary, you can never achieve anything purposeful with it save for phones, fast-moving women and cars."

Senator Adams nodded at those words, "Which is why I said the whole country, and the educational system, need to be revamped. It's high time we told kids that the essence of going to school is to acquire knowledge and skills, not just certificates. We need to let them know that paper won't open doors and even when it does, the door can only remain open when they possess the necessary skills and knowledge."

"You are totally right about that," Ekwueme said in agreement. "Our society used to place more emphasis on certificates, but now, it's a different ball game and these kids need to learn. Besides, it pays to make legit cash. Aside from the fact that you will get to sleep with both eyes closed and without worries, you will also get to experience life beautifully, gain insights, and more knowledge. Those three ingredients will only pave a way for expansion and more money."

"Exactly," Senator Adams concurred. "I remember when some of my friends at the university decided to go the other way and amass quick wealth. I won't say I am a saint though. I joined them, but only for a few months. My mother's advice kept ringing in my head. I could clearly hear her telling me that it's not the best way to live life or make money. I had to go back and think, and I realized that way of life was not who I wanted to be, and it's not the kind of life I wanted to live. I cut off from those friends. Today, two of them are in prison and it pains me to think about that, because they were brilliant," he shrugged. "They are even lucky to be alive; some died while living that way. Trust me, the first thing I teach my kids whenever I wake up in the morning is not to engage in anything that I wouldn't be proud of when I hear it and if I ever ask them to do something wrong for money, they should stand their ground and say a firm 'no' even to me."

The senators, including Ekwueme, nodded as he spoke. Ekwueme's mind also drifted back to some of his friends who decided to take the quick route out of poverty and as expected, the wealth was only for a while—it did not last.

The rising voices from the dining room made the senators stop their conversations. Ekwueme excused himself to find out what was going on. He knew Ebony and Ejiofor were not on good terms, but he had no idea they would go as far as arguing in less than four hours of meeting each other again.

"You have to eat this food," he heard Ejiofor say. "I won't touch it if you don't. I'm serious about it."

"But I made it for you," Ebony protested. "Just eat. It's nice."

On sighting Ekwueme, they both kept quiet and looked away from each other.

"What's wrong?" Ekwueme asked, keeping a neutral expression.

They both refused to say a word and that irritated him the more. Ekwueme narrowed his gaze on his younger brother. "Is the food not good or what, Ejiofor?"

"It seems it is," Ejiofor replied. "But I haven't even had a taste. Ebony served the food and kept watching me. That made me cautious, so I asked her to taste the food before I eat it."

Ekwueme was visibly angry. "Why would you do that? She went as far as making the food by herself for you and that's how you appreciate her?"

Ejiofor looked up at his brother. "I am sorry, brother," he said, "but I won't touch this food until she eats from it. I have my doubts. I know

Ebony better than you do and she's not the kind of righteous person you think she is."

"What's your problem?" Ekwueme yelled at him.

Ekwueme had become angry with his brother, but he decided to settle it amicably and then call his brother to order later. For God's sake, Ebony was not just a stranger in the house, but a woman he was getting married to in less than a month. The sooner his brother accepted that, the better for everyone.

"Dear," he called, looking at Ebony. "I know this is ridiculous, but please, for my sake, just have a taste from the food so that peace can reign. Or do you want me to have a taste of it?" Ekwueme stirred it.

"Don't taste it, brother!" Ejiofor screamed.

Ebony fidgeted, with her feet shaking, and Ekwueme sensed it.

Ebony's hesitation to have a taste of the meal surprised Ekwueme. "Darling, please," he urged her, before turning to Ejiofor. "As for you, we will talk later. I don't know what has gotten into you, but you need to end it. You are not getting any younger. Despite your level of exposure, you still behave like you did fifteen years ago. I will not tolerate this kind of behaviour from you anymore. I have guests in my house, for crying out loud."

"I'm sorry, brother," Ejiofor said. "But she should just taste the food, if you truly want me to eat it."

"Ebony?" Ekwueme called again. "I would not subject you to humiliation, ever. But please, just this once, kindly taste from the food."

"But you know I don't eat semolina," Ebony protested despite looking scared.

"I know," Ekwueme said. "Just a morsel will do."

"I..."

"Just eat it," Ejiofor interjected. "You made the food, so eating should not be a problem. Contrary to what you think, I appreciate you for going out of your way to cook for me. It's not every day someone gets to witness such an act of kindness from you."

"Ejiofor, keep quiet when I'm talking to my wife. Please," Ekwueme frowned at him before turning to Ebony. "Darling, please, just a taste. Or is there something you are not telling me?"

She shook her head. "Nothing."

"Then taste the food," Ekwueme pleaded. One look at him could tell that he was starting to get tired of the cat and dog fight between Ebony and Ejiofor. "Ebony?"

Ebony stood rooted to a spot and tears welled up in her eyes. Ekwueme could not believe his eyes. "Ebony, eat the food," he said, as calmly as he could.

She made no move to have a taste and that was when Ekwueme started to get suspicious. He stared at Ejiofor, who had this triumphant smile on his face. He turned back to Ebony, she was shaky and sad.

Ekwueme shook his head and walked out of the dining room without another word at any of them.

CHAPTER SEVEN

Senator Ekwueme walked out of the dining room in fury. A deep scowl was on his face when he entered the living room. The look on the faces of his guests told him that they could tell he was angry, but he cared less. He made no attempt to hide his anger.

"What's wrong?" Senator Adams asked with a concerned look.

"It's Ejiofor and Ebony."

"What happened?" Senator Adams inquired.

Ekwueme went on to narrate everything, including how Ejiofor had asked Ebony to taste the food, how she refused, and how he was tired and left them to sort out their issues.

"Something is definitely fishy," Senator Adams said.

"True," Senator Ezeuwa affirmed.

"I'm done trying to settle those two," Ekwueme said in anger. "They can do whatever they deem fit."

"Let's see what the problem is," Senator Adams said, standing up. "This is one of those things that come with getting married and having a third person from either of the families living with you. You just have to be a man and sort it out before everything gets out of hand."

The other senators joined him and together, they walked into the dining area. Ebony and Ejiofor were still there, just the way Ekwueme left them.

'This must be serious.' Ekwueme thought.

"Young man," Senator Adams called, "you do realize that she is your brother's wife-to-be and it's high time you accepted her, right?"

Ejiofor smiled and turned to him. "I'm sorry, sir. This might sound rude, but the only thing I want her to do is to taste this food she gave to me," he said. "I've known her for a very long time now, and I know what she is capable of. If she can't eat this food, then I'm not going to touch it."

"This is no way to treat your brother's wife-to-be," Senator Ezeuwa cautioned Ejiofor.

Ekwueme stood in silent observation, irritated by the scene. He turned to Ebony; she had tears trickling down her cheeks and he instantly felt sad for her. He imagined how bad he would feel if he had a taste of the way Ejiofor treated her.

Ekwueme turned to Ejiofor; he wondered what must have gone wrong with his younger brother who used to be kind and loving.

"Ejiofor," Ekwueme finally called. "Just eat the food, please. We will trash whatever issue you have with Ebony later. I don't like this sort of scene you are creating."

"I'm sorry about the scene, sir," Ejiofor apologized, but one look at his face told Ekwueme that he was far from being sorry.

"Eat the food, Ejiofor or you leave it." Ekwueme turned to Ebony. "Come with me."

Ebony and Ekwueme made to walk away, but Ejiofor stood up and walked past his brother.

"Ejiofor?" Ekwueme bellowed.

"Sir," he answered, pausing in his track. "I want to go back to my room."

"What is even wrong with you? Do you think you are still seventeen or what?"

"Sorry, sir," Ejiofor said, slightly bowing. "All I want is for her to taste from the food, or else I won't touch it. Why would she give me food and stand behind me, waiting to see me eat? That's how people are poisoned in Nollywood dramas."

The other senators opened their mouths in shock. Ekwueme was disappointed in his brother. If Ejiofor were still younger, he would not have hesitated to slap him for uttering such words.

"Are you sure you're okay, Ejiofor?" Ekwueme was boiling in anger. The level of disrespect stunned him. He knew that if he did not make efforts to pluck Ejiofor's wings, he would relax, start to fly and dish out more disrespect. Heck! He might even beat Ebony up. "She is not your plaything, she's the woman I'm getting married to. Get it into that thick skull of yours."

Senator Adams walked to Ekwueme and held his hand, "Calm down," he said. "These things happen. For peace to reign, she should just taste the food. Later, you should talk sense into your brother."

"Eat what food?" Ekwueme asked in anger, still staring at Ejiofor. "She's not eating anything! What sort of disrespect is this? If he's not hungry, then he should go and sleep."

Senator Adams tried to calm Ekwueme down, but he was not having any of it. Obviously, he had had enough of Ejiofor's childish display.

"Let me talk to you outside for a minute," Senator Adams muttered.

Ekwueme exhaled deeply and followed Adams to the other end of the living room.

"This is not the way to handle this kind of thing," Adams started. "Allow her to taste it. Later, you warn your brother to desist from doing such. Supporting her in this manner will only breed more hatred in your brother's heart. Once he hates Ebony, I give you my word that he will make every other member of your family hate her too. Just reconsider your stance on this."

Senator Ekwueme nodded in agreement. The last thing he wanted was hatred and division in his family. Of course, he understood the kind of responsibilities on his shoulders as the first son of the family.

They walked back and joined the others. Ejiofor was now seated on one of the chairs in the dining room while Ebony still stood with tears running down her cheeks. Senator Ekwueme had sympathy all over his face as he looked at her, but he was left with no choice. "Ebony, please taste the food," he said to her.

"I...I... I don't like semolina," she stuttered.

"I know. Just take a little of it," he urged.

"Ebony, I'm sorry this is happening," Senator Adams said. "But please, for peace, just eat, maybe one handful." He folded his fingers to demonstrate what he meant.

Ebony shook her head. "I... I can't."

"What do you mean you can't?" Senator Takwas queried.

"See?" Ejiofor clapped his hand happily. "She cannot taste even a little from the food she gave me. You people should ask her what she added in it."

"I didn't add anything," Ebony said, her voice shaky.

"Then, taste it!" Ekwueme's voice rose a notch higher. "Ebony?"

With more tears running down her cheeks, Ebony continuously shook her head in protest whimpering like a bird beaten by a stormy rain. "I can't."

The other senators started to murmur and that was embarrassing to Ekwueme.

"Ebony, at least taste the food!" Ekwueme commanded. He no longer cared if she was his fiancée or a stranger. All he wanted was to put an end to the scene before him.

"But I can't!" She sobbed.

"What did you put in the food?" Ekwueme screamed at her.

"I didn't put anything in it."

"Then taste it," Ekwueme took out his phone, "or I will call the police."

"Don't," she cried. "Don't please."

"Young woman," Senator Adams said. "Why not save yourself these tensions? It will not take anything from you to taste the food you cooked. What exactly is the problem?"

"Oh please, please. I usually don't like semolina." she began to sob loudly.

"I'm calling the police," Senator Ekwueme said, as he started to scroll through his contact list for the DPO's mobile phone number.

"Oh, no. No. Do not call, please. I will confess. Please, let me confess."

All eyes turned on Ebony in confusion.

"Confess?" Ekwueme asked just to be sure his ears were not playing pranks on him.

"Yes," Ebony nodded as her cries increased. "Please don't call the police."

CHAPTER EIGHT

The word 'confess' shocked everyone in the dining room. They had not seen it coming, but since it was out already, they all stared inquisitively at her, frowning in anticipation of her confession.

Ebony had tears smeared all over her face. "I will talk," she said. "It's not my fault."

"What's not your fault?" Ekwueme yelled at her. "What are you even talking about?"

"I tried to settle things with him, but he refused. I..."

"Calm down, Ebony," Senator Adams cut in. "Why did you say you will confess? We only asked you to taste the food you gave to Ejiofor."

They all stood there with their eyes fixed on her, but she was too ashamed to talk. When she did what she did, she never envisaged this sort of outcome. Now, everything was a big mess. For the second time in one day, she wished the ground would open and swallow her.

Tears trickled down her cheeks and she bowed in shame. Ebony wished she had not acted on the idea when it crossed her mind. All she ever wanted was Ejiofor's silence concerning her past life. She was not the sort of 'demon' Ejiofor thought she was, and she had tried her best to make him see that, but when he did not pay attention to her pleas, she had embraced the only alternative she had.

"Ebony!" Ekwueme screamed, forcibly pulling her out of her thoughts.

Shivering, she looked up at him. "Yes?"

"Answer the question," he calmly told her.

Ebony sniffed. She wished she could disappear.

"Ebony, answer them," Ejiofor sneered.

She could not look at his face, but the mockery was evident in the tone of his voice. Without being told, she knew he was smiling inwardly at his success. She wished she could blame him for pushing her to the wall, but the deed had already been done. She had to bear her cross alone without apportioning blames to anybody.

She recalled the first month she met Ekwueme. He had told her to bare her all to him. She wished she had listened because if she had, she would not have found herself in this sort of mess.

"We are still waiting, young lady. What is it you want to confess?" Ayomide reminded Ebony.

"Her sins, of course," Ejiofor taunted. His excited tone rang in Ebony's ears.

"Ebony, we are waiting to hear what you have to say." Ekwueme persuaded her, ignoring his brother's arrogance.

"I...I...I..." she stuttered.

"You what?" Senator Ekwueme and Adams asked in unison.

"I poisoned... I poisoned... the soup," she murmured before bursting into fresh tears.

The senators were speechless in the room which was silent as the grave.

Ejiofor had to break the silence. "I knew it!" He got to his feet. "I knew you had evil intentions towards me from the minute you set your eyes on me today."

While Ejiofor was speaking, Ekwueme had his head buried in his palms. The senators all stared at her with different expressions that screamed disbelief.

Ebony cried profusely as she stared at Ekwueme. The minute his hands left his face, she went down on her knees.

"I'm sorry, it was not my intention. I tried to plead with him not to spill the secrets, but he refused to listen."

Ekwueme shook his head. "Ebony, did I offend you?"

Ebony shook her head. "You didn't. I'm really sorry." She cried.

Ekwueme walked past her and hurried towards the kitchen. "Where did you get poison in this house and where did you keep it?"

Every other person followed suit, leaving Ebony who was still on her knees.

"Ebony, is it not you that I am talking to? Where is the poison you put in the soup?" Ekwueme growled at her.

Ebony stood and slowly made her way into the kitchen. The tears in her eyes clouded her vision. She wished she could turn back the hands of time. She wished she had allowed Ejiofor to spill the beans instead of attempting to kill him. She felt dirty for thinking of such an evil act.

She could not blame her being desperate, even if she could; Ebony knew nothing would save her from this mess.

Ekwueme opened the tall kitchen cabinets. "Where is the poison, woman?" He yelled at her.

"It's not there," she informed him. "It's…"

She had barely finished when he interrupted her with another scream. "Are you going to talk, or should I call the police to bundle you out of my house?"

"Please, don't," she cried, kneeling again. "I will talk. I poisoned the soup with a flower."

"Flower?" Ekwueme's eyes dilated with pain and fear.

The other senators started to murmur.

"Yes," she stammered, wiping her nose with the back of her palm. "I put a little of the dieffenbachia flower at the back of the door."

"What?" Ekwueme barked.

Ebony could tell he was confused. "It's a dangerous flower that kills fast. I only added a little quantity to the soup."

"You are wicked!" Ekwueme said in a cold tone. "How could you? I mean, I loved you so much and I gave you the freedom to come to me with whatever issue you had. Even if your heart was that bitter towards Ejiofor, you could have brought whatever it was to me and we would have sorted it out."

Ebony's heart sank. True, she should have taken that approach, but in her moment of confusion, she had taken the step that seemed the easiest. She cried loudly when she looked up at Ekwueme and saw the tears in his eyes.

"I'm sorry," she pleaded.

"Sorry doesn't fix anything," Ekwueme shot back at her. "What is it that you had against my brother that made you decide to end his life?" He stared pointedly at Ebony, waiting to hear whatever she had to say.

"I know a lot about her hideous past." Ejiofor said.

Ebony lowered her tear smeared face. "I've changed. It was just a little mistake. I regret my past. I wish I could go back and live a better life. I tried to tell Ejiofor that I am no longer the kind of girl he used to know, but he refused to listen to me."

"You have changed but you decided to kill him?" Senator Adams asked. "Over that little thing?"

"He said he would never allow me to marry his brother while he was still alive," Ebony told them.

Ekwueme turned his eyes on Ejiofor, and then back to Ebony. "So, what secret do you have that made you want to commit murder?"

Ebony refused to talk. The tears kept flowing…

"Don't worry," Ejiofor said, smiling. "I will tell you who your beloved fiancée used to be and how she lived her life like there was no tomorrow," he turned to Ebony. "Don't worry yourself, I will tell the story for you since you don't want to talk. I still remember your dirty past vividly."

Ebony felt defenceless. All she could do was cry and wish that Ekwueme would forgive her after listening to what Ejiofor had to say.

"Please, can we all go back to the sitting room? You may need to sit down because my story will definitely take a while," Ejiofor pleaded with the senators.

Without a word, the senators started back into the sitting room. When Ebony did not follow them, Senator Adams went back into the kitchen and made her get into the sitting room.

Senator Ekwueme was lost in a deep dark well of sorrow, and the sadness that enveloped him broke Ebony's already fragile heart. Ejiofor took the seat facing his brother and started to narrate their story right from when they were both in class one in secondary school.

At this point, Ebony was not so sure her relationship would survive Ejiofor's onslaught. Everything that happened seventeen years ago was fresh in the minds of Ejiofor and Ebony, as though it had only happened yesterday.

CHAPTER NINE

On a Monday morning, Ejiofor scurried to the huge brown gate of Umunuhu Secondary School with a big signboard bearing the school's name in green paint and bold letters.

Ejiofor walked into the premises dressed in a green short and a sparkling white shirt, well tucked in. Beyond the gate were five small buildings scattered in the premises; all painted green and white, like every other government-owned secondary school in the state.

After he had dropped his schoolbag, the morning assembly bell rang out and the students started to converge at the assembly ground. Ejiofor took his backpack and sauntered to the assembly ground immediately.

Everything about him screamed focus and brilliance. He barely paid attention to the school prefect's order to hurry down to the assembly ground as his eyes were busy scanning the surroundings. He kept looking until he found what he was searching for.

His heart leapt in excitement and a tinge of happiness swept across his face. His steps quickened. At thirteen, Ejiofor was one of the most brilliant students in class one. His grades were outstanding, likewise his character and appearance. He barely talked to anyone, so it came as a shock to his classmates when he became friends with Ebony. Not that he was a snob; he was the typical definition of an introvert—he always kept to himself and rarely engaged in any school activity except it was compulsory.

"Hi Ebony," he said, walking closer to where she stood with two other girls. "How are you?"

"I'm fine," she answered.

He arched his eyebrows at her. She understood the signal and said a quick goodbye to the girls.

"I brought something for you," he informed her as soon as they were out of earshot.

"What did you bring this time?" she asked, all smiles.

Ejiofor laughed. Since they became friends, he had grown fond of bringing her little gifts almost daily. He was that caring. Whatever he laid his eyes on that appealed to his senses and was affordable, he usually bought for her.

This time, he fished out four udara (African Star Apple) balls and handed them to her. "They are all yours,"

"Thank you so much, Ejiofor."

Ejiofor nodded. The smile on her lips and the radiance on her face whenever he gave her those little gifts was the most important to him. The smile showed she liked whatever he gave, and he loved it when she appreciated or commended his effort.

The bell rang out again. She made to leave, but he held her back. "I didn't say you can go."

"This is the third bell. Any moment from now, those prefects will start punishing us." The look on her face showed she was less than pleased with the prefect's actions.

"I know," Ejiofor said, rummaging his backpack. "Found it!" He took out a beaded bracelet and gave it to her.

She danced in pure delight.

A prefect bellowed at them and they hurried towards the assembly ground. They soon parted ways as both genders had to stand in their designated lines.

Ejiofor could not stop thinking about Ebony and the way she had danced in joy when she saw the bracelet. He knew he already achieved his primary aim for the day. Their eyes met briefly, and they smiled at each other before Ebony turned to focus on the instructions the assembly prefect was rephrasing.

Ejiofor sighed. If he were not in the same class as her, he would have long asked her out. He could not blame God or his parents, but he wished he could turn back the hands of time and enjoy his childhood, go to school with his mates and just have fun like every young kid without worrying about constant sickness and ill health.

His mother had often told him that among all her kids, he was the one with the weakest immune system. If he had not been sickly, he would be in class three with his age mates and he would have been able to ask Ebony out without fear of Ebony turning down his advances.

He was still deep in thoughts when a prefect came to stand beside him and tapped his shoulders. "Where's your beret?"

"Sorry, I forgot to wear it," Ejiofor apologized, opening his backpack. "It's in my bag."

The school's green beret was one of the things Ejiofor hated the most. It had its place in his bag, and he only wore it whenever he was on the assembly ground or whenever a prefect walked into his class. He just did not like caps—beret or face caps, he was not a fan.

While searching for the beret, he realized that the milk-like juice from the udara fruit had stained one of his book covers—it totally ruined it.

The sadness on his face only lasted for a minute. For Ebony, he would do anything. He quickly separated the book from the others and made a mental note to re-wrap it with another cover. He wrapped all his books with colourful magazines. It was not stressful to get wrappers because his father was an avid collector of magazines and newspapers.

He fished out the beret and quickly wore it. "I found it!" He enthusiastically informed the prefect who would not stop staring at him with a scowl.

"The next time I see you without your beret, I will seize the beret," the prefect warned before walking away.

The assembly began, but Ejiofor was far from being present. He kept throwing glances at Ebony and daydreaming. The previous day, Ebony had told him that she hoped to become a lawyer when she was older; the news had gladdened his heart because he hoped to become the Central Bank Governor. He had thought they would make a perfect combination.

He did not need anyone to tell him that he had fallen head over heels in love with Ebony—his friend from way back. Yes, they had known each other long before secondary school. The secondary school only reunited them; it was not the beginning of their friendship.

He clearly remembered when they were younger and their mothers had sold foodstuff at Umunuhu Local market every Afor market day. They used to play together and go in search of grasshoppers while their mothers were busy. The adventure came to an abrupt end when Ejiofor's mother decided to go back to school for a teacher's training course.

Ejiofor was sad, but being a kid, he soon forgot about Ebony, made other friends and continued with his life. It was on the fifth week of resumption that the headteacher brought in a girl and told everyone that she would be joining their class.

At first, he did not recognize her. After all, as a child, he only had a mental picture of an angel of about six years old whom he craved to see again. Although he could not deny the fact that she looked familiar from the minute he set his eyes on her. It was the following day when the class teacher came in for a roll call that he knew she was Ebony. The realization hit him and immediately the class teacher left the class, he walked to her and introduced himself. It took her a while to recall who he was, but she finally did. That was the beginning of their reunion. It had started out as a harmless, normal friendship. But as time progressed, Ejiofor could tell that he was in love.

Being in love was one of the things he did not look forward to, until the day he first walked into the school. His intentions were clear— focus and study hard to impress his elder brother who was paying his school fees. Then eventually become the Central Bank Governor.

Ejiofor took one last look at Ebony who was already absorbed in the on-going assembly activities, before gaining focus. *Let's see how things will go between us.'* He concluded in deep thought.

CHAPTER TEN

Ejiofor and Ebony's friendship blossomed to the extent that they were always together. Wherever you saw one, you would definitely find the other. In no time, everyone in the school came to know about them. Some students envied their friendship while some others openly called them 'love birds.'

Ejiofor could not deny the fact that he was in love, he knew that he would be staking too much by asking her for a relationship at his young age. He wondered how it would feel if she turned down his request? That would automatically bring an end to their friendship. It was something he did not wish for. He enjoyed her company and that was what mattered.

On Tuesday morning, Ejiofor walked into the school premises. Joy was written all over his face when he spotted Ebony sitting at a secluded corner of the school.

It was unusual. Since they became close, she was always by the gate every morning, waiting for him; then they would both walk to the classroom or assembly ground, talking and laughing.

Ejiofor walked towards her and on getting closer, he noticed the frown on her face. It broke his heart to see her that way.

He drew in a deep breath, mustered enough courage, and covered the remaining distance between them. "Ebony?"

She turned to him with a smile, but Ejiofor was not a kid, he knew a feigned smile when he saw one.

"What's wrong, Ebony?"

"Nothing is wrong," she responded, shaking her head.

"You know you can always talk to me, right?"

"It's nothing."

Ejiofor shrugged. There was no use pestering her. If she wanted to share her problems, she would have spilled her worries even before he asked. Nonetheless, he was surprised by this new behaviour. They had shared and talked about everything, ranging from personal secrets to number of admirers, and many topics. He wondered what could be so personal that Ebony did not think she could share with him.

The sound of the assembly bell pulled him out of his thoughts.

Ebony got to her feet. "Let us go to the assembly ground."

"You still don't want to tell me what is wrong?" Ejiofor asked. "Is your mother sick or something?"

Ebony shook her head. "Nothing. I was just thinking about life and why things happen the way they do. That's all."

Ejiofor was not convinced by her response. Sure, he had also thought about those things a few times, but he had never looked that sad. Again, he didn't think such things would bother a carefree person like Ebony.

They walked to the assembly ground in silence, which was also odd. They usually talked and laughed their hearts out whenever they were together.

The morning assembly came to an end thirty minutes later and every student left for their respective classes. Ejiofor was searching for Ebony amongst the crowd when he saw her walking away with some girls in their class.

It broke his heart. He had always known he would make a jealous lover, but he did not think he would be that broken by Ebony's action. He walked dejectedly to the classroom.

Ebony spoke to Ejiofor the moment he walked into the classroom. "Ejiofor, I searched for you. Where were you?" She managed a tight-lipped smile in his direction. He did not need anyone to tell him it was a lie. Something was definitely wrong somewhere. She knew where he always stood. If she wanted to walk with him to the class, she would have waited for him to meet up with her—there was no need for any search.

Ejiofor walked to his seat, maintaining a smile. He watched Ebony converse with the other girls in the class. Her eyes were everywhere except his direction. He was bothered, as it was the first time, he would be that worked up over a girl. He ransacked his thoughts for what could have possibly caused the rift between them.

Ejiofor pondered if they had had any form of disagreement on Monday. He shook his head because there had not been any event as such. Everything was fine between them. So, what happened between Friday evening and Monday morning to make Ebony ignore him in that manner?

He was still brooding when he noticed Davies, one of his classmates, who strolled into the class holding a phone to join Ebony and her clique. Davies was the only boy in their class who owned a mobile phone. As a result, many of the girls fawned over him.

It was a disappointment for Ejiofor to see that Ebony had become one of those girls. He would have said something to her, but the mathematics teacher walked in and learning activities for the day commenced in full. Ejiofor barely paid attention to what the teacher was saying. His mind was preoccupied with the change in Ebony.

Ebony, on her part, barely looked in his direction. Even when it was time for lunch break, she did not go to his seat as she usually did, instead, she went with the girls, and they all left the class with Davies, laughing excitedly.

Ejiofor did not go out for lunch. He was too weak to do so. Again, he did not want to bump into Ebony and her group where they were probably laughing and hanging on to every word Davies said, as if their lives depended on it.

"Ebony," Ejiofor called, as soon as she walked back into the classroom.

"Hi Ejiofor," she answered nonchalantly and turned back to her group—her new friends.

If Ejiofor thought her earlier actions broke his heart, then her nonchalance shattered it into a thousand pieces.

The previous week, they were 'love birds' and now she was acting like she barely knew him. It took everything he had in him to stop the tears from escaping his eyes. At the expense of being embarrassed by her friends, he walked up to her and tapped her shoulders. "Can I talk to you?"

Ebony looked at him for a while before she nodded in agreement. "Sure!"

Ejiofor led the way and they went back to his seat. He heard the other girls giggle and gossip.

"What did I do to you?" he asked, without mincing words.

"What?" Ebony laughed. "You haven't done anything wrong to me."

"Then, why are you avoiding me like a plague?"

"I am not avoiding you. If I was, I won't be talking to you. I am just hanging out with girls for a change."

"Is Davies a girl?" Ejiofor shot back at her. "Is he?"

She giggled. "He was showing us something on his phone."

Ejiofor shook his head. "You can go back to your friends."

She left and he lowered his head to his desk. The fact that she was laughing all through the conversation with no atom of remorse in her tone, made him feel worse than he had felt earlier.

In the weeks that followed, there was no positive change in Ebony's attitude towards him. Instead, it got worse. She was always in the company of her new friends and Davies. She barely paid attention to him and she started to despise whatever gift he bought for her, considering them cheap.

She even went as far as making demands and telling him what to buy and what not to buy. It pissed Ejiofor off, but then, he was young and in love, and he wanted to please her even if it meant making himself unhappy or uncomfortable.

Ejiofor sadly realized soon enough that the main cause of disaffection was the fact that Davies had a mobile phone while he did not have.

Whenever he tried to talk with her, she would give him the excuse that she was busy checking out something on Davies's phone.

For the very first time in his life, Ejiofor wished he were from a different home—a rich one. He wondered what it would feel like to have rich and generous parents like Davies. Davies' father was an Ivory Coast based businessman and he never looked back whenever he wanted to spend on his family, especially his only son, Davies.

Davies had a chopper bicycle, an elegant school bag, he dressed neatly and now he had a phone. A lot of the girls wanted him around too as he often bought them snacks during lunch break.

Whenever Ejiofor heard Ebony's laughter, it hurt his ears. He did not need confirmation that she was 'checking out' something on Davies's phone.

He sat in class one day and lowered his face as the tears welled up in his eyes. He wished his parents were rich enough to afford him a phone.

CHAPTER ELEVEN

It was a month and two weeks. Ejiofor had lost some weight from watching Ebony and the other girls frolicking around Davies. She paid him no attention and only talked to him whenever she needed answers to an assignment or classwork. She would then take the answers to her group and share it with them.

Ebony's action angered Ejiofor, but he did not want to do anything that would fuel the already burning fire. He followed the logical approach and gave her whatever she asked. Their friendship became a parasitic one of taking without giving, but he did not care, he still enjoyed seeing her smile whenever he granted her request.

On one occasion, during the break period, he confronted Davies and asked him to leave Ebony alone.

"Is Ebony your wife or personal property? Let her be." Davies blasted.

"She's my friend. You caused the rift between us."

Both of them exchanged expletives, starting with Davies who made fun of Ejiofor's dark complexion.

The exchange was almost degenerating into a fight as Ejiofor grabbed Davies's collar and turned him around.

Davies laughed. "I will eat you up like ripe mango if you don't leave my neck now. Lovesick boy. I would find another friend if I were you."

Just then, Ebony walked up to them, grinning. "What is going on, boys?"

On seeing her, Ejiofor immediately let go of Davies.

"Nothing," Ejiofor quickly said. "I was just trying to correct his mistake."

Davies hissed. "He was telling me he doesn't like how close we are." The ridicule in his voice discomforted the already embittered Ejiofor.

Ebony shook her head at Ejiofor. "It's not fair. Davies is a good person and I can be friends with anyone."

It was painful to hear the mockery in Davies's voice, but it was even more painful to hear Ebony take sides with him.

"Don't worry, we shall see." Ejiofor said and walked away.

Three days before the incident with Davies, Ejiofor had tried talking Ebony into going back to the way they used to joke and laugh with each other, but she gave flimsy excuses, saying she needed female friends in her life because there was a lot to learn from them.

Ejiofor had no issues with her female friends, his problem was Davies who seemed to have started touching Ebony in an indecent manner. It broke his heart, but he was helpless.

By the following Friday, Ejiofor approached Ebony a few minutes to closing hours. "Let's leave together when the bell goes off," he suggested.

Ebony shook her head in refusal. "I have things to do."

Ejiofor nodded and went back to his seat. She had formed the habit of staying back with her friends and Davies. Ejiofor could not bring himself to imagine what they did in school after closing hours.

On his way back home that same afternoon, he made a stop at the local market to find out how possible it would be to please Ebony—if he still had a chance with her. He stopped in front of a mobile phone shop and stared at the packs of phones on display. When he saw the exact phone Davies had, he nodded in satisfaction and walked in.

"Good afternoon, sir," he greeted the phone dealer who happened to be a man in his mid-twenties, "please, how much is that phone?"

The phone dealer's eyes followed the direction of Ejiofor's pointed finger. "That one?"

Ejiofor nodded. "How much?"

"Eight thousand naira."

Ejiofor's eyes widened in shock. It was difficult for a boy his age to have eight thousand naira.

For such a small device? To make calls and play games?' He thought, clearly bewildered by the cost of owning a mobile phone. "I will come back when I have the money. I just wanted to make enquiries." He left without waiting for the seller's response.

As Ejiofor walked home, he could not stop thinking of ways to please Ebony. He had her best interest at heart, but clearly, he could not afford to buy her a phone.

The next day, being a Saturday, Ejiofor had to wash his father's clothes. It was part of his chores. While at the task of washing clothes, he saw some naira notes in the back pocket of one of his father's khaki trousers. He took them to his father.

Mr Nick Isiawele was delighted. "Thank you, son," he beamed at Ejiofor. "I didn't even know I left such money in my trousers. I forgot."

Ejiofor nodded and went back to his chores. He knew his father was a bit forgetful and did not attach so much importance to money. It was not the first or even the tenth time he was returning money found in his father's pocket.

The following Monday morning, he dragged his feet to school—he barely paid attention to his other classmates who beckoned on him to walk faster so he would not be late.

"I'm fine," he told one of them. "Today is just one of those days when I don't feel like going to school."

The classmate shrugged and left him.

Everyone dreaded being punished for lateness on a new weekday, but Ejiofor cared less. He preferred the strokes from the teacher's cane to seeing Ebony in the company of those girls and Davies. By the time he got to school, the morning assembly had ended and students were scurrying to their classes. He narrowly escaped the cane.

In class, he had to bear the sight of Ebony with her clique again— not that he had a choice anyway. They were classmates, but they grew further apart daily, and Ebony did not seem bothered.

During lunch break, Ejiofor walked up to Ebony. "Hey, can I talk to you?"

She stood still for a while with her eyes fixed on him. Ejiofor concluded that she was probably thinking up another flimsy excuse and braced himself for it.

"Go ahead," she said.

Ejiofor could not believe she agreed to speak to him.

"Are you going to speak, or will you keep staring? I have only a minute before I leave the class with my girls."

"Oh, okay. I just wanted you to know if we are still friends," Ejiofor said, his tone sad and sober.

Ebony laughed. "Yes, we are," she took Ejiofor's hands. "Davies has lots of interesting things on his phone, and he lets us use it whenever we want. That's why I am hanging out with him and the girls."

"I see," Ejiofor muttered.

"You should join us," Ebony suggested, and Ejiofor instantly snatched his hands from hers.

"You can go with your friends," he mumbled.

She bounced off without another word.

"So, the phone is the issue here?" Right there, he vowed to get her a phone.

On the Saturdays that followed, he started to keep whatever money he found in his father's pocket while washing his clothes. For him, it was a good thing he had always returned his father's money. No one, not even his father, would suspect anything was missing or that he took the money.

Ejiofor's plan was to get Ebony a phone from the money he stole, so he prayed that his father would never find out, else, he would be doomed.

CHAPTER TWELVE

Exams began. Ejiofor had always been a brilliant student, but his obsession with Ebony and the emotional trauma she was putting him through made it very difficult for him to pay attention in class, let alone read his books. Nobody knew this. He was more concerned about how to complete the money he had gathered so far for Ebony's phone.

A few weeks after exams, their third term results were out. Ejiofor's result brought him nothing but sadness, coupled with how bad he already felt from all of his problems with Ebony.

He fought hard to control his tears as he unfolded the result sheet and stared at it again, hoping the scores would change. After several seconds of unwavering stare, he realized that they would never change. This was real, not a dream. He had placed tenth in a class of thirty students. How it happened, he could not tell, as he felt he had done his best to read for the exams.

In the previous terms, he had retained the first position. He remembered how happy his father was on those two occasions. The mere thought of how his father would feel when he saw the result in his hands made him cry.

He walked to the mango tree beside his class and sat under it, wondering what he would do with the result. He could not tear it or do something silly with it. His father would kill him if he found out.

In the end, he had no choice but to take the result home, to his father. He figured that telling his father that the result collection was postponed was not a good idea because his father was quite familiar with some of his teachers and he would ask questions.

As if having a bad result was not enough, he got home and found his father seated on his favourite chair right outside the house.

"Ehihe ọma, nna m," Ejiofor greeted. He hastened his steps and made to run inside the house.

His father's voice stopped him in his tracks. "Ejims, where is your result sheet? I've been here waiting patiently to rejoice over your result."

Ejiofor's feet lost their strength. He turned slowly, with guilt written all over his face. "I ... I ..." he stuttered.

"I thought you went to school to get your result?"

Ejiofor reluctantly walked back to his father, took out the rumpled result sheet, and handed it to him.

Mr Isiawele carefully wore his glasses and peered at the result sheet while Ejiofor shivered beside him.

"Ejiofor, what is this?" his father scowled and stretched the sheet to him.

"I'm sorry, sir," Ejiofor said, with a shaky voice. "I don't know what happened. I read for all the subjects."

"If you read, what then happened?" Isiawele growled, taking off his eyeglasses. The frown drew a series of contours on his face. "This is the last time you'll come back with this kind of result."

"It will not happen again, sir," Ejiofor assured his father, but one look at his father told him the elderly man was less than convinced.

Ejiofor expected such a reaction. His father had always been an ardent lover of education and for him, any position less than the first was as good as outright failure.

"Ejiofor," Isiawele called again, "tell me what happened this term."

It was one question that even Ejiofor could not answer.

"Go inside." Isiawele ordered.

At that point, fear gripped Ejiofor. The last time he was instructed to 'go inside' he ended up receiving six strokes of cane.

Ejiofor dropped to his knees and took a praying posture, "Father, I'm sorry." But it did not look like Isiawele cared.

"Go inside," he repeated calmly.

Ejiofor staggered into the house while imagining the cane hitting him hard on his back. His mother tried to welcome him, but he only managed a quick greeting in her direction and walked unsteadily into his parents' bedroom.

He stood, regretting why he ever bothered so much about Ebony and her new friends. Now he was about to receive the beating of his life and none of them was there to help him.

Few minutes passed and he heard his father's footsteps approaching. Ejiofor's heartbeat doubled. He silently prayed to God to forgive his sins and soften his father's heart towards him. The door opened and he was soon standing face to face with his father and mother.

"What are you doing here?" Mr Isiawele asked.

"You asked me to come inside," Ejiofor reminded him.

"Ehen, is this your room?"

His father's statement shocked him. Ejiofor's earlier fear turned into excitement and he hurried out of the room immediately, running past his parents, though he heard his father complain about his poor performance to his mother. He heaved a sigh of relief when he stepped into his room.

The following day, Ejiofor went about his duties as if he did not come home with a 'horrible' result. His father had neither made mention of the result nor did his mother.

On the third day, while he was relaxing under the mango tree in the compound, his father came home, furious. Ejiofor greeted him, but he paid no attention to him as he walked into the house. Ejiofor wondered what was wrong. He certainly did not think he was responsible for the anger.

"Ejiofor, come here!" His father screamed from inside the house.

He dropped the basin of orange in his hands and rushed into his parents' bedroom. He held his hand on his chest to calm his breath, "You called me, father."

"Sit down," his father ordered. "Do you mind telling me what happened to your result? I mean the truth."

At that moment, Ejiofor knew he was in trouble. "I... don't... know," he stuttered.

"I met with your class teacher and he told me that Mazi Okonkwo's son came first in your class. I am just coming from their house. The boy said you got distracted by a girl called Ebony."

Ejiofor's eyes nearly popped out from their sockets. Everyone in his class knew he no longer talked to Ebony, so how could Somadina tell his father that Ebony distracted him? He was furious and felt bad that someone could go that far to taint his image. "Father, it's a lie."

"So, what pushed you from the first position, to tenth? Do you have a better explanation?"

Ejiofor scratched his head. He wished he had a better explanation.

"Mazi Okonkwo's son said you were always talking and laughing with the Ebony of a girl whenever any class was going on. Ejiofor, you are only thirteen, what is your business with a girl?"

Ejiofor could not say a word.

"I am disappointed. Leave my room before I descend on you."

Ejiofor bowed his head in shame and walked out of the bedroom. He was the sole cause of his problems. If he did not put all of his energy into thinking about Ebony and trying to find a way to get her a mobile phone, he would not have found himself in such a dilemma.

His mind drifted back to Somadina's betrayal. How could he? They were neither friends nor enemies, so how could he say such a thing to his father? Ejiofor had never looked down on Somadina, neither had he ever tried to paint him black before anyone, which was why he thought his actions were uncalled for.

After much thought, Ejiofor concluded that Somadina's intention was to make him look bad before his father. He made a mental note to deal with Somadina whenever he crossed paths with him.

He resolved to read during the holidays to impress his father and prepare ahead of the new class. He already had someone who was willing to lend him some old class two textbooks.

CHAPTER THIRTEEN

During the one-month holiday, Ejiofor was the best version of himself: sweeping, reading, washing clothes and even carrying out chores that he was not asked to, all in a bid to impress his father and make him forget the result. But because he realized he still loved Ebony and still needed to get her a phone; he did not stop picking money from his father's pocket.

The night before resumption of the new school term, Ejiofor sat in his room in deep thoughts. A new term was beginning, a new class too. He knew he could not afford to make the mistake of returning home with any other position than first. He did not need anyone to tell him that his father sparing him once did not translate to being spared a second time. Once bitten, twice shy. *I need to put extra efforts into my studies,'* he concluded.

Just then, he heard his father call his name. Ejiofor knew what it was. He had been expecting it all evening.

"Sit," his father said.

Ejiofor did as he was told even though he was sure he could predict half of all his father was about to say.

"You are going back to school tomorrow morning." Mr Isiawele started. "With your raging hormones and the current level of exposure in the world, I know you will be feeling like an adult and raising shoulders because you are in Junior Secondary School 2 (JSS 2). Here's what you don't know: you have a whole life ahead of you. You turned 14 last month and you would probably live until you are 80. When you subtract 14 from 80, you will know that you have not even started on this journey called life.

You see that thing that happened last term? I do not want a repeat of it in this house. You are too young to be bothered by girls or relationships. Face your studies, grow older, work hard and make a name for yourself and girls will chase you. Don't try to open a pot on a hot stove to taste the food in it because it will burn you. I don't want to hear about you getting distracted over any girl again."

"I won't, sir," Ejiofor promised.

Inwardly, he knew there was nothing his father would say to make him forget Ebony. She already had her place in his heart.

"You can go to your room now. Make sure you wake up early to prepare for school. I don't want you starting the new term with lateness."

Ejiofor nodded and left the living room.

Back in his room, he draped the bed cover over his body, thinking about how he would behave when he saw Ebony the following morning and it was not long before he drifted to sleep.

A cockcrow woke him at dawn. Rubbing his sleepy eyes lazily, he climbed down the bed and walked towards the kitchen. It was a chilly September; he needed to boil water for bathing.

An hour and thirty minutes later, Ejiofor was set to leave for school. He went to his parents' room, bade them farewell and left.

As expected, the first person he noticed amidst the crowd of students was Ebony. What was more surprising was the fact that she came to meet him after their eyes met.

"How was the holiday?" she asked.

"Fine." Ejiofor could not believe his eyes—she was smiling and talking to him just the way she used to before Davies' less-than-exciting entry into the picture. "How was yours?"

"Very fine," she stretched her hands tiredly. "I enjoyed the one-month break, but I missed my friends, including Davies."

Ejiofor hissed softly. *'Oh, no! Here we go again. On the first day of school?'*

Ejiofor wanted to ask if she missed him, but decided it was best to let a sleeping dog lie. Even if she did, she missed Davies and his phone more.

"What did you do during the holidays?" He asked.

"Ah!" Ebony screamed excitedly, looking over Ejiofor's shoulders. "Davies is here. See you later. Bye."

Ejiofor felt like someone pricked his heart with a pin. Hot tears gathered in his eyes. The dying passion to get a phone was once again rekindled.

After the morning assembly, they started with an introduction from the new class teacher. Then the classes officially began with the mathematics teacher introducing them to trigonometry.

It was fun, especially for Ejiofor who paid full attention to all that was being taught. He could not imagine letting his father down again.

When school closed for the day, he walked to Ebony's seat and asked if she would like to leave with him. She declined his offer with a smile. He did not bother asking why because he knew the reason—another hangout with Davies, his phone, and her loud female friends.

For the next few weeks, he received the same treatment from Ebony, but he never for once thought of hating her or being rude to her whenever she came around to collect a note or a pen from him. It was what their friendship had become, and he had no choice other than to live with it.

"What if I got you a phone?" he asked Ebony one Friday after the morning assembly.

She turned to him, wide-eyed. "You mean it?"

He nodded. "I want you to be happy," he said, but all he wanted was for her to quit following Davies around like her life depended on him.

"Wow!" She briefly hugged him. "I will be so happy if you do that."

Ejiofor was happy to see her that way. At home, he already had close to ninety percent of the money that was needed to get the phone, all he needed was three or four weeks to get the balance.

The following Saturday morning, he joyfully took out his father's clothes for washing, knowing that before the end of the day, he would have gotten some extra money. Luck shone on him and he found two crumpled five hundred naira notes in the back pocket of his father's trouser.

He quickly pocketed the money and continued washing, singing and whistling. After washing, he packed the buckets and went inside.

"Did you find any money in my trousers?" his father asked, startling him. "I am looking for a thousand naira and it seems I left it in one of the trousers you washed."

Ejiofor shrugged. "I didn't find any money. Check your room very well, maybe it fell somewhere."

He dropped the buckets close to the bathroom where they belonged and left for his room. His heart continued to beat fast. He was still rejoicing over the new addition to his wallet when his father walked in.

"Ejiofor Isiawele, did you say you didn't find any money in one of the trousers you washed?"

Ejiofor shook his head with his hands held up. "I didn't see it o. If I had, I would have returned it to you."

"I am asking you for the last time, did you or did you not find money while washing my clothes?"

Ejiofor felt the heat run down his face. Was his father suspicious?

He dismissed the idea. There was no way his father would suspect him. He was very forgetful and he had earned his trust. Encouraged by that thought, Ejiofor, again, denied finding any money.

"Kneel!" His father ordered in a calm, yet angry voice.

Ejiofor clenched his hands. "Daddy, I am saying the truth. I didn't find any money. You know me. I would have returned it."

Isiawele shook his head. "I don't know this new you. I intentionally put that money in that pocket. It was bait and you fell for it. I have been doing that for a while after I noticed you've stopped returning money to me after washing my clothes. I am truly disappointed in you, Ejiofor."

Ejiofor started to shed tears. His father just caught him in the act and there was no way out. Worst, he could never tell his father why he stole all the money, so he opted for the only viable option, which was pleading for forgiveness. "Daddy, I am sorry. I promise, I will never do it again," he said as he went on his knees.

"Keep your 'sorry' to yourself!" his father screamed at him. "Your elder brother will hear about this. Ejiofor, I have always done my best for you and have never denied you anything, why did you choose to start stealing from me? Why? Tell me, what do you do with the money?"

Ejiofor bowed his head. He cannot tell his father the truth, "I am sorry."

"Sorry for yourself!" His father stormed out of the room without another word.

Ejiofor burst into tears. His father had promised to tell his brother, and it was something he did not want for himself. He knew his brother would be terribly disappointed in him and might beat him up badly.

"God, what did I do to myself?" Ejiofor murmured, crying like a baby.

CHAPTER FOURTEEN

Waking up every morning and watching other young people walk past his house on their way to school was pure emotional torture on Ejiofor. He regretted his act. He wished he could turn back the hands of the clock. He wished his father would pardon him. Instead, his father asked him to think if he would like to continue school or if he would prefer learning a trade.

The latter was not an option, not even in his wildest imagination. He had always dreamt of becoming a Central Bank Governor, there was no way he could achieve that by learning a trade. Ejiofor wanted fame, and for him, there was no better way to achieve that than having his name, picture or signature circulate all over the country, wherever naira is spent.

He sobbed as he watched the early morning school rush. He would have been amongst them if he had not nursed the idea of getting a phone for Ebony. He recalled all his plans to grab the first position for himself in that term and sobbed more.

Apart from the fact that his father seized every dime he had saved and reported him to his brother, Ejiofor was under house arrest for two weeks: no school, no church, no market, no strolling around. All he could do was come out to the veranda or run minor errands that did not involve money.

Every minute of his existence was filled with regret. *'Had I known!'* Sure! If he had known he was going to get caught, he would have dismissed the idea long before he had the chance to put it into action.

He was still brooding when he heard his name. Ejiofor left the veranda and rushed towards the kitchen.

Since the incident, he had become soft, overly obedient, and never tried to argue with his parents no matter how hard the chore or task was. He went about his duties diligently.

He was like the repentant thief on the cross; he needed no soothsayer or preacher, he simply advised himself and turned a new leaf. He stepped into the kitchen and met his mother dishing out food.

"Yes, mother," he played blind to the plate of yam porridge on the kitchen counter. Food was not his problem. School was.

Ejiofor wished he would be given the opportunity to go to school for just one day in a week, he did not mind going on an empty stomach.

"Your food," his mother announced, pointing at the plate.

Ejiofor leaned against the kitchen wall with his expression soft and sober. "I'm not hungry."

"Don't even let me start with you," his mother pointed a finger at him. "Take your food to the living room and eat. *Osiso!*" Her eyes were full of anguish.

"I'm not hungry," Ejiofor insisted.

"Ejiofor Isiawele," she called, sternly, "you are looking for trouble."

Ejiofor knew that already. He had refused to eat the previous night as well, but then, his mother had ignored him. Who would not refuse food after one week of not going to school? He knew how much of his plans were going down the drain because of the punishment. On several occasions, he had thought of pleading for forgiveness, but his father's facial expression scared him. No doubt, he was still angry about the whole thing.

"Mother, I want to go back to school," he cried. "I'm sorry. I won't steal again."

"Ejiofor, until you tell me the truth about what you were doing with such a huge amount of money, you are not going anywhere."

Uh-oh! That was top secret. Telling his parents that he was stealing from them just so he could get a mobile phone for a girl would stop his entire schooling. He was remorseful and had made up his mind never to steal again, but he was not so sure he could tell them such ugly truth.

"Mommy, please help me beg father. I want to go back to school. I'm missing a lot of teachings."

"You didn't know that when you started stealing from your father?"

Mrs Isiawele hissed and walked out of the kitchen.

Ejiofor burst into tears. He knew he could not afford to miss another school week. One had passed already. Throughout the previous weekend, he had looked forward to, and even imagined his father calling him to his room and telling him he had forgiven him.

Ejiofor sat on the floor, sobbing. Until he met Ebony, he had never played with his studies; he loved school, he adored his teachers. He was working towards his dreams and aspirations.

A few minutes later, his mother returned to the kitchen, carrying an empty plate. "Ejiofor, warn yourself," she wagged a finger at him. "Don't let me pour my anger on you."

"I'm sorry," he muttered. "Please, help me plead with dad. It will never happen again. If I ever do it again, he should stop me from going to school forever."

Ejiofor meant those words. He liked Ebony, but his schooling was more important. He felt his heart constrict in his chest when thoughts of Ebony flashed through his mind. She was probably laughing and throwing her body on Davies.

The first day he missed school, he had half-expected her to show up in his house to find out why he was not in school. It was a new week already and he had given up the thought. It truly showed how much she cared about him.

"Ejiofor, where did I fail in raising you? Who taught you to steal? Who?" His mother asked.

"Nobody." Without thinking, he did the only thing that crossed his mind: kneel to plead for forgiveness.

"Then how could you do such a thing?" Her voice went cold.

"Please forgive me," he pleaded. "I will never do it again, I promise. I will never. Please trust me again, please."

"Stand. I will plead with your father on your behalf. But if this repeats itself, I will make sure you drop out and become an apprentice at that roadside mechanic's shop close to your school. That way, all your classmates will see and laugh at you."

Ejiofor's heart leapt in joy. The first part of his mother's words was all that made sense to him. The other part would never happen because he would not be so foolish again to let it happen. Finally, he would go back to school. He was sure because his father had never declined his mother's request.

He ate his breakfast and did all his chores while waiting for his father to come home. When his father got back in the evening, he quickly greeted him and scampered for safety just as he had been doing since the past week.

He was not sure how long it would take for his mother's charm to work, so it came as a huge surprise when a few minutes later, his father bellowed his name.

He ran into the room. "Sir?"

"Your mother tells me you want to go back to school?"

His father's stern look did not deter Ejiofor. "Yes, sir. Please, sir," he said, getting on his knees.

"Are you sure?"

Ejiofor nodded. "I'm truly sorry for stealing your money, it will never happen again."

"I see you've repented. I forgive you."

Ejiofor was glad to hear those words. He jumped for joy. "Thank you, father, and thank you, mother."

"Remember this, Ejiofor. If you want to be the best at what you do, look for something that makes you happy and focus on that. If education is what you want for yourself, focus on it and forget about every other thing going on around you. If it's a trade or a skill, go for it."

"I choose education, sir. Thank you, sir,"

"You can go."

Ejiofor nodded and ran out of the room excitedly. He wasted no time in fixing his uniform, school shoes, and books, in preparation for his return to school.

CHAPTER FIFTEEN

Ebony's friendship with Davies progressed as the days went by. They became inseparable. It did not take long before their classmates started calling them names like 'love birds' and 'black lovebirds', just like they did when she was close friends with Ejiofor. Ebony was happy with her new life and friendship. Davies was always willing to get her whatever she wanted for lunch and even after closing hours, they stayed back in school and played together.

Since their friendship blossomed, they started walking to school together. They had a spot under the udara tree by the bush path next to the main market where they usually met. Ebony was always the first to show up, then she would wait for at least five minutes before Davies arrived.

That Tuesday morning, while she waited, she could not help but think about Ejiofor. Since their first term in class one, he had never missed school for one day. She wondered what happened. How could he stay a whole week without bothering to show up in school? It was unlike him.

She shrugged. As much as she hoped he was okay, a week without Ejiofor meant a week of chatting and playing with Davies without any sort of interruption.

"Ebony!" A male voice called.

She turned to see Davies approaching. "You are early today; you look happy too. What's happening?" She asked.

Davies laughed. "I'm always happy. Thanks for waiting for me."

He held her hand and together, they started towards the school.

"It's a new week," she said, looking up at him. "You promised to get me a phone, remember? One that looks exactly like yours."

Davies scratched his head. "We will talk better during lunch break. I promise I will get you the phone soon." She nodded.

They walked the remaining distance in silence. Ebony could not wait to hold the phone in her hands; she wished it would come faster. Since Davies made the promise, she had spent days imagining herself owning and holding a brand-new phone. She had a lot of things to do with it, ranging from games to pictures, to sending a lot of messages to people just like Davies always did. Ebony wanted to live in her own virtual world where no one could access.

On reaching the school gate, she was shocked to see Ejiofor. As usual, he was dressed in his clean shorts and sparkling white shirt. Ejiofor smiled at her, but she only managed a tight-lipped smile in response. She was with Davies, and there was no way she would leave him to talk with Ejiofor.

As usual, she noticed the disappointment on Ejiofor's face when she walked past him to their classroom. She had enjoyed one week without his face haunting her and she only wished he would stop it.

Ten minutes before the morning assembly bell rang; Davies left her side to speak with some of his male friends. She used the opportunity to walk to Ejiofor's seat.

"How are you, Ejiofor?" she asked, smiling.

"I'm fine."

He did not smile back, but she cared less. They were still friends, even though they were not as close as they used to be.

"I'm glad you are back. But, why did you miss school for one week?"

"Nothing," he answered.

"You missed a lot," she said, sitting next to him. "Mr Nnabugo almost gave an impromptu test. He was teaching the different aspects of trigonometry and he felt we were not listening, so he asked us to tear out a sheet of paper and that the test was going to be five marks. We pleaded with him and he cancelled it. He also said that you are his best student and he didn't want you to miss any test."

"Thank you," Ejiofor turned to her. "I see you're still friends with Bonjour."

"Who's Bonjour?" Ebony asked in pretence.

"Davies looks like the boys in a pirated French book." Both Ejiofor and Ebony laughed out loud.

"Davies is a nice person. I don't know why you don't like him. Davies has never stopped me from talking to you or any such thing, he's a good person. I'm still trying to build my friendship with him and that's why you always see me with him."

"So, that's a yes?"

The morning bell sounded and Davies chose that moment to return to the class in his usual demeanour, as if he owned the school. Ejiofor stared at him angrily.

"I have to go," Ebony said, getting to her feet. "I'm glad you are back."

She left him and moved to join Davies.

"I came to call you so we can go to the assembly ground together," Davies said, taking her hand.

"Sure."

They walked out, leaving Ejiofor to stare at them unhappily.

Minutes later, the assembly began, but Ebony could not concentrate on what was going on. She kept throwing glances at Ejiofor who would not stop staring at her. It made her uncomfortable. She wished he would understand that there was nothing she could do—she valued her friendship with Davies more.

Davies listened to her more and was always willing to provide whatever she wanted. Besides, he had promised her a phone and she was looking forward to getting it. She could not trade all of that for anything.

The assembly came to an end without her grabbing anything that was said. As usual, she waited for Davies so they could walk to the class together. Instead of Davies, Ejiofor walked up to her.

"Let's go to the class together," he told her, smiling. "I have missed laughing and talking with you."

Ebony shook her head. "I have missed it too, but I'm sorry, I'm waiting for Davies." She looked over his shoulders. "Oh! Here he comes."

"No problem," Ejiofor grumbled and walked away.

She turned to look at his retreating figure and murmured, "Sorry. There's nothing I can do about this."

"Ejiofor is disturbing you again?" Davies inquired, as soon as he reached her.

"He wanted us to go to class together," Ebony informed him.

Davies laughed and took her hand in his. "He's lovesick, he likes you."

Ebony slightly punched him on his shoulder. "We are just friends."

"He doesn't see you as just friends, he likes you. But," he turned to her. "I like you more. I will get you the phone soon. Not just that, I will get you any other thing you ask for. All you need to do is ask."

Ebony giggled excitedly. "I think I like you too. But get the phone first, it is more important to me. Anything else can follow later."

"Sure!"

Owning a phone in class two? What more could she ask for? She did not need any further convincing; Davies was an angel and she was happy to do whatever he wanted in exchange for the phone.

CHAPTER SIXTEEN

Ejiofor walked home with a sad face. He was sad because his one-week absence strengthened the bond between Ebony and Davies. Clearly, she did not care if he stayed at home for one month without coming to school.

Unfortunately for him, he was no longer thinking about getting her a phone because he could not risk a repeat of the last incidence with his father, but he was more concerned about getting her to see that he still cared despite all her misdoings.

"Davies doesn't deserve you, Ebony," Ejiofor murmured.

On reaching home, his mother had his food ready, but Ejiofor had no appetite. He covered the food, went to the kitchen, and put it aside. Food was not his problem, Ebony and Davies' friendship was.

Due to the one-week absence, he had collected some notebooks from his classmates to update his notes, but with the kind of mood he was in; he could barely pick up a pen, let alone write.

"Ejiofor!"

He heard his name and lazily walked to the kitchen. "Mother?"

"Why didn't you eat your food?"

"I'm not hungry. I will eat later."

His mother's expression swiftly changed. "What happened? Are you sick?" She touched his forehead and ran her hand down the side of his face.

Ejiofor shook his head. "I'm fine."

After much pestering from his mother, Ejiofor ate the food, but that was the last meal he ate for that day. He was too bothered about Ebony and Davies.

Throughout the night, Ejiofor had his mind focused on how to get Ebony to end whatever she had going on between her and Davies. He was not rich and certainly did not own a mobile phone, but he could tell that she was way happier with him than she was with Davies.

Late at night, an idea crept into his mind. He toyed with it and realized that it was a good one. With that, he drifted off to sleep.

The next morning, he went to school earlier than usual hoping to be in class whenever Ebony walked in with Davies.

While he waited, he updated some of his notes with the topics he missed. He knew how his teachers were and knew they were going to start demanding for complete notebooks whenever exams approached.

When it was time for assembly and Ebony had still not shown up in class, he became worried. As he walked to the assembly, Ejiofor silently prayed for her wellbeing.

At the assembly ground, he found Ebony and Davies. He smiled at her, but she turned away. He felt his heart shatter but maintained decorum and moved to his own side of the assembly line.

Ejiofor barely paid attention to what was going on until the assembly came to an end. He sighed in relief and silently walked to the classroom.

A few minutes later, Ebony walked in without Davies by her side. He saw it as an opportunity to execute the plans he had in mind.

He left his seat and stepped to her. "Hey, Ebony."

"Ejiofor," she answered without glancing at him.

"I got something for you," he informed her, hoping he could get her attention.

She turned to him and shook her head. "I'm not interested."

Ejiofor felt hot tears fill his eyes. "You didn't even ask what it was."

She turned to him with a frown. "Is it the mobile phone you promised?"

"No." He shook his head. "It's fruits."

A small chuckle escaped her lips. "Ejiofor this is no longer JSS 1, people are upgrading gifts. They now give out mobile phones. I don't want your fruit. Thank you."

Her nonchalance angered Ejiofor, but he kept it to himself. Replying her in the same tone and way she talked would foil all his plans. "It's okay if you don't want it."

He went back to his seat. A teacher strolled in and the day officially began.

While the class was going on, he threw glances at Ebony. He kept thinking of ways to get Ebony to see that he truly cared about her. Before the second class was over, he got another idea and decided it was best to implement it during lunch break.

Ejiofor fixed his stare on the classroom's wall clock at any opportunity he had. He wished for time to move faster and prayed his plan was successful at lunchtime.

Lunch break finally came, and Ejiofor could not be more excited. He waited for the rowdiness in the class to die down, but while at it, Ebony walked out of the class with Davies holding her hand. For the third time in one day, he felt his heart shatter to pieces.

Ejiofor went back to his seat and rested his head on the table to hide his tears. He wished he were rich; that way he could have Ebony to himself and buy her whatever brand of mobile phone she wanted.

Ten minutes before lunch break was over, he could not sit still anymore. He wandered out of the classroom in search of Ebony. *'I will tell her how much I care about her. I don't care if I get laughed at.'* Ejiofor thought. He went to the school's canteen, but there was neither sign of Ebony, nor Davies.

After scanning the surroundings with his eyes and not finding her, he decided to look for her in the library. It was unlikely that he would find her there as she was not much of a studious student, but he decided to check anyway. She might want a quiet place to sit with Davies and the library was the best spot.

Unfortunately, he did not find her. His next stop was the science laboratory, but again, his efforts came back fruitless. Ejiofor gave up on his search and was on his way to class when he bumped into Enyioma, his classmate and new friend.

"I've been looking for you, where did you go?" Enyioma asked.

"I was searching for Ebony," Ejiofor replied, stepping out of his path.

"You are still a JJC. Your one-week absence made you miss out on a lot of things," Enyioma smirked.

The smirk on Enyioma's face aroused Ejiofor's curiosity. "How do you mean?"

"You are the only one in this school who doesn't know what's going on between Ebony and Davies."

"I don't understand." Ejiofor wished Enyioma would get rid of that silly look on his face and just go straight to the point as his heartbeat already tripled due to suspicions.

"Those two love birds usually go to the Agricultural Science teacher's farmland close to the school canteen, during lunch break. He would then buy her snacks and drinks whenever they come out."

"Tell me you are lying."

Enyioma laughed. "Stay there and be depressed over a girl while she's having fun with another guy. I'm sure you already know what they go there to do. If you like, don't wise up."

Enyioma laughed and walked away. Ejiofor was angry, pained, and terribly annoyed. He remembered the disappointment on his father's face after he was caught stealing. He remembered how angry his mother was and it brought tears to his eyes. A girl he was doing all of that for and was still willing to walk the length of the earth for her sake, was busy messing up with another boy just because he had a mobile phone?

Ejiofor wiped his tears and went to the classroom. He decided he would carry out his own findings to know if this was true.

Chapter Seventeen

Ebony felt satisfied and happy. She dusted dirt off her skirt and shirt. She wiped sweat off her face and smiled over the fact that she was few steps to getting her dream mobile phone. The saner part of her conscience pricked her, but she waved it aside. After all, people say that one needs to give what one has in exchange for whatever one wants.

She was giving what she had and paying the needed price for something she desperately needed. Davies was such a wonderful person and she could not have picked any other above him. Who would not pick the richest and most generous boy in class?

The previous week, he got her a dress and gave her some money for her personal use. Who else would do such for her? Nobody. She was glad he picked her over every other girl in school. It was a dream come true.

"Are you okay? You seem worried," Davies asked as they walked out of the farm, hand in hand.

"No, I'm fine."

He was so observant and always made sure she had a smile on her face whenever she was around him. He was exactly the kind of person she had always wanted. Now that she had him, she would never allow Ejiofor to come between them.

She once gave Ejiofor all her time, but now, the tone of the music was different. He could never provide all that she wanted, and she did not want to waste her time with him while every other girl in class was having fun buying the latest shoes and clothes.

"Smile," Davies said, looking down at her with a smile etched on his own lips.

Ebony smiled at him and they kept walking. She remembered when their friendship progressed to the phase it was. Davies had assured her that he was going to make sure that no one got hurt in the process. True to his words, he had been doing a lot to make her happy, even though there were days he did the exact opposite of making her happy. She did not care though, and she did not need a soothsayer to tell her that she was paying the price.

"Ebony, I like you a lot, your smile makes me go gaga and I'm going to make you happy. Forget all about Ejiofor and just roll with me. I promise you won't regret this, ever." Davies assured her for the umpteenth time in one day.

"I know. Why do you think I'll still be thinking about Ejiofor?"

"I don't know. Maybe because you're unusually quiet," Davies revealed.

"Oh, no, I'm not thinking about him. He's not even worth a thought."

"Okay then. I believe you."

They got to the school canteen and Davies asked her to mention everything she needed for lunch so he would get it for her.

She made her request and he did not hesitate to get everything. Some schoolgirls threw side glances her way, but she cared less. She was with the richest boy in class, so why should she pay attention to the people who were jealous of her?

From the canteen, they walked to the classroom with Davies holding her right hand while she steadied her backpack with the other hand.

Before she became friends with Davies, there was absolutely no need to go for lunch break with her backpack, but now she had to, because inside the backpack was a wrapper which was a necessity for the new path their friendship had taken.

Just outside the classroom, Davies stopped to have a brief chat with some of his male friends.

"You can go inside, I will join you later," Davies said to Ebony.

She nodded and walked in. The first person she caught sight of was Ejiofor, as he sat dejectedly with his head bowed. It was like magic, but the moment she fixed her gaze on him, he looked up and hissed.

'What's wrong with him?' She wondered. He had never given her such a hostile stare before. Why should he be annoyed?

He had been in a good mood before she went out for lunch break. She briefly looked around to see if something like a fight had happened in class while she was away, but she realized there was none: no scattered chairs, no black eye on anyone's face, and no single scratch on his body. Ebony shrugged and went to her seat. She had more important things to worry about than Ejiofor's mood swing.

She took out the snacks and started munching. Halfway into her lunch, she saw Ejiofor walk towards her and she quickly braced herself for another unsolicited gift or interruption. She had long realized that whenever he marched that way to her seat, he usually came with a lot of questions.

"What did you go to the Agricultural science teacher's farm to do with Davies?"

Ebony gently placed her snack on the desk and looked up at him. "Ejiofor, what's the meaning of that question? And who told you I went to the farm? Can't I go out for lunch break again without problems and gossip?"

"So, you don't know this leaf followed you all the way from the farm?" Ejiofor revealed by pulling a small piece of cassava leaf from the buckle belt of her backpack. "Can you deny it now? Ebony, is this what you have become?"

Shame washed over Ebony. But she quickly hardened her heart against any regret or show of emotions.

"The last time I checked, Davies is my friend, just like you are."

"Are you really sure I'm still your friend?"

"Well, that decision is up to you. If you don't stop harassing me, I'll stop being your friend."

Ejiofor sat on her desk and stared at her face. "This new life you are living is not going to help you in any way. I still want to hear it from you, what do you always go to that farm to do with Davies? I heard from some people in the class that you've been going there every break period since last week."

'Enyioma.' Ebony thought. *'That talkative is at it again.'*

"Davies is my friend and we can go anywhere we choose. Are you my father, or what?" She raised her voice and closed her eyes, "Who the hell are you to me? You better stop poking your stinky nose where it doesn't belong."

"Ebony, where and when did I offend you? I gave you everything I could provide. Don't tell me it's because of a common phone that you are doing all of these things with Davies."

"Ejiofor, you call it common. Okay, tell me, where is your own?"

"Do you expect me to rob a bank to get a phone or what?" He shot back at her.

"Then stop calling it common," she rolled her eyes. "Please leave, I want to eat my food in peace without being interrogated."

"Ebony, we ..."

"Stop it! Allow me to breathe some fresh air," she exploded, with a note of finality.

CHAPTER EIGHTEEN

Ejiofor walked back to his seat with slumped shoulders. The new Ebony he just spoke to was a disappointment. His heart ached badly; he wished he did not even come to school. His heart and body would have been safer at home than having to watch these heart-wrenching scenes and listening to talks about Ebony and Davies' escapades.

Even the less observant student could notice that Ejiofor's body was just present in the class while his focus and attention were absent. He had daydreamed at long intervals, carrying his chin on his palm and engaged in deep thought.

For the next couple of hours, Ejiofor could neither get his thoughts together nor focus on what his teachers were saying. While he sat on his chair, he was tempted to cry. Davies and Ebony would not stop staring and smiling at each other at every opportunity.

It pierced Ejiofor's heart to see them that way. His thoughts were in complete turmoil and to cover up, he ground his buttocks on the chair.

Ejiofor literally had a thousand and one questions running through his mind when the elderly mathematics teacher, Mr Nnabugo Thomas, stepped into the class to announce that they would be taking his test in two weeks' time.

While he was at it, Ejiofor noticed the teacher's stare on Ebony. At first, he frowned at the realization and waved it off as nothing. But when it persisted, he turned to look at Ebony. For once, she was not making fun with Davies and her entire focus was on the teacher until he left the classroom.

He heard Enyioma and some other boys in class talking about how a teacher had caught Ebony and Davies and promised to report them to the school authorities if they do not stop their stupid activities on the farm and even in the classroom.

Ejiofor wondered about what he witnessed. Everyone knew how notorious the mathematics teacher was with the female students. Was he on to Ebony too? Was he the teacher Enyioma had talked about? Or was there something else he was missing?

Home Economics was the last class they had for the day and Ejiofor could not wait for it to be over so he could head home and try to forget his pains. Unfortunately, the teacher, Mrs Onwuka, noticed his absentmindedness halfway into the class. She was in her late fifties and wore glasses but still, all the students knew she was an eagle-eyed fellow. No tiny detail passed by without her noticing it.

"Ejiofor!" she called, forcing him out of his reverie. "You are not listening to me; instead, you're lost in thoughts."

Ejiofor looked up at her in confusion. How did she know? He thought he hid the fact that he was not listening perfectly well. He had his eyes on her even though he could not understand a thing from all she said.

He nodded and sat up like a kid caught stealing cookies. In a moment, he lost himself in the thoughts of Ebony.

"Ejiofor!" the teacher called again, startling him. He saw her standing beside him, and had no idea how she got there.

"What was the last sentence I made?"

Ejiofor had confusion written all over his face. He could barely remember the topic, not to mention the last sentence. He racked his brain, trying to see if any of the things she had said since she walked in, was imprinted somewhere in his memory. After a few seconds of trying, he gave up, looked up at the teacher, and shook his head.

"Meaning?"

At the sound of that, he knew he was in trouble. A huge one. Tears formed in his eyes out of fear of what punishment she would give him. Mrs Onwuka was one of the loveliest teachers they had, yet the strictest. How did he not remember that earlier? If he had, he would not have attempted to touch the lion's tail.

"I'm sorry, ma," Ejiofor pleaded, making a pitiable face with hope it would help to soften her heart. "I have forgotten."

"You forgot? Ejiofor, you used to be the brightest student we had in junior class, what is happening to you?"

"Nothing, ma," Ejiofor answered, wishing he could say exactly what his problem was. Well, his problem was sitting at the other end of the class staring at him.

"If nothing is your problem, then tell me what the last statement was about," Mrs Onwuka insisted. "Or, you forgot that one too?"

Ejiofor nodded. "I'm sorry ma. Henceforth, I will pay attention to all you will teach."

Mrs Onwuka shook her head at him and grimaced. "I am very disappointed in this new you. You had better change. If not for your past records, I would have sent you out of my class. An elderly woman like me is on her feet, teaching, while you, a kid is relaxing in his seat thinking about all the nonsense you children do now."

Ejiofor nodded like an obedient student while wishing the class would end, so he could move on to other things. Mrs Onwuka left him and went back to the chalkboard while Ejiofor wore back his thinking cap. Their school was the only secondary school in the community and the schools in their neighbouring communities were not within walking distance. If it was not so, he would have found a way to convince his father to change his school. Now that changing school was not an option, the only option he had was to endure whatever sight he had to see or just ignore them.

Ignoring them would have been the best, but he noticed that since she said those harsh words to him during lunch break, she had started to rub her friendship with Davies in his face. Whenever a teacher left the class, she would go over to Davies' seat, which was right behind her seat. She would laugh loudly just to make sure Ejiofor heard it.

Ejiofor was the most excited student when the closing bell rang. He picked up his bag and left the class before anyone else. He heard someone scream his name, but he kept walking without bothering to find out who it was. Although, he had his suspicions from the tone of the voice. There were only two people who had such a deep voice in his class.

"Won't you wait for your girlfriend today?" Enyioma teased, panting.

"Enyioma, stop it!" Ejiofor shot him a warning stare.

"Ejiofor, you need to stop this too," Enyioma taunted, walking beside him. "You almost fell into Mrs Onwuka's trap because of Ebony. You are lucky. If she had decided to punish you, trust me, Ebony would have been the first to laugh at you."

Ejiofor frowned at him, still angry. He was right about that. Ebony would not have hesitated to fill the whole class with her laughter, especially now that she hated him and was doing everything to impress Davies. She might have added something to mock him, afterwards.

"Ejiofor, you need to forget about that wayward girl," Enyioma advised. "Life is in stages. At this stage, a girl should be the least of your problems, no matter how beautiful she is. If all of us were to be attracted by beauty, that means all the boys in class would be dating Ebony or Chiamaka. They're the most beautiful girls in the class. If you try to harvest a premature mango and eat it, the tartaric acid in it might burn your lips or your organs."

"What's your point?" Ejiofor grumbled. He hated proverbs because his father had a proverb for every situation, and he was tired of them.

"Leave Ebony alone and focus on what brought you to school," Enyioma said. "My elder brother would always tell me that when I become rich, famous and successful, women will be the ones chasing me. But most importantly, people will respect me. That is why you see me studying hard and trying to up my grades in every term. I can't wait to grow older, make a positive impact in society and live comfortably."

Ejiofor knew that Enyioma was saying the truth, but he also knew it was not as easy as he said. Unless he woke up with amnesia, there was no way he would just forget her. He knew it was going to take a while. The good news was, he was willing to put in whatever efforts needed to break the bond between him and Ebony.

CHAPTER NINETEEN

In the days that followed, Ejiofor became a shadow of himself. Watching all of Ebony's transformation made him sick to his stomach. In class, she barely paid attention to what any teacher taught. She either spent her time whispering and laughing with her seatmate, or she was sleeping in class. Whenever the teachers tried to caution her, she would complain about feeling feverish.

Ejiofor knew she was lying; he did not feel an iota of sympathy towards her. How would he? She practically ripped out his heart from its place and shattered it on the cold floor.

With Enyioma's assistance, Ejiofor put the ugly experience behind him. By the start of a new term, he was way over Ebony. Although the first weeks were not easy, he was able to ignore Ebony's excesses. But he failed to ace his exams. He studied his books but could not assimilate because the thoughts of Ebony kept infiltrating his mind.

For the second time, he had to endure the pain of seeing his father's disappointed expressions. His father almost slapped him when he found out that Somadina had come first for the second time. Luckily, his mother had been there to plead on his behalf and encouraged him to sit up because she would never plead again if he came home with such terrible results in the term that followed.

Disappointing his father and himself was not as painful as hearing Somadina telling another classmate that Ejiofor was chasing skirts. Ejiofor had rushed in and attempted to hit him, but the other students held him back and asked Somadina to stop poking his nose where it does not belong.

Ejiofor was boiling with rage. When Somadina told his father the same thing when he had bagged the tenth position, he had forgiven him because the anger had died down after the one-month-long vacation. But with his recent remark, Ejiofor did not think he would forgive. He was determined to get back at Somadina and the only way he could was to secure the first position for himself.

To worsen the situation, Somadina and Davies were now the best of friends. Ejiofor was not surprised anyway. Birds of a feather flock together.

Friday of the eighth week of school was full of lessons and for the first time since his ordeal with Ebony, Ejiofor was hundred percent focused in all his classes. He took down notes as well as points from the teachers' explanations.

At the end of the day, the closing bell rang. Impulsively, he turned to Ebony's seat and realized that she was deeply asleep. How could one person be sick all the time? The Ebony he knew never got sick. Ejiofor quickly waved off the thoughts of her.

He looked back when he saw Mr Nnabugo approach Ebony and wake her up. She peered at him and smiled like the happiest person on earth. Ejiofor had long gotten over her, but with what he saw, he felt his heart constrict. Nnabugo was one of the most popular teachers in the school, but unfortunately, he was popular for the wrong reasons. His promiscuity was a known fact.

Ejiofor's hand went to his chest, trying to still it. So, the rumours were right? Ebony and Nnabugo now had a thing going on. Ebony and a grandfather?

Several times, he heard students whispering about the relationship, but he did not want to believe it because he did not think Ebony would stoop that low to have any sort of relationship. Any responsible girl who cared about her body and wellbeing would never go close to Nnabugo except for necessary academic reasons.

Now that the evidence stared him in the face, Ejiofor was utterly disappointed in Ebony. How did she go from a beautiful good girl to a spoilt child in the space of one year?

Did it mean she no longer had anything with Davies? Or, were the rumours lies?

He noticed the decline in their laughter and talking, but Ejiofor had thought they were getting tired of gossiping and mocking people. So, someone had come in-between them? It was good news to Ejiofor's ears. He knew about the law of karma and he knew that every action came with a consequence. He was living the life with Ebony when Davies snatched her attention from him, now the same thing had happened to Davies.

Ejiofor did not see that coming because Davies was the richest kid in their class, but whichever way, he was happy that Davies would finally know what it meant to have something of value stolen from him.

Ejiofor walked home, took his bath, and decided to nap, but the image of what he had seen remained etched on his mind. He tried to shake it off, but his efforts bounced back. What could Mr Nnabugo have promised Ebony that made her fall easily into his trap? What was the bait?

The next morning, Ejiofor walked into his class and met an uproar. Ebony's voice was the loudest and it caught his attention. He turned to see what was going on, surprise registered on his face when he saw her holding a brand-new phone—the exact kind of phone he had made enquiries about in the market.

Ejiofor shrugged. Either the mathematics teacher or Davies must have got it for her, no doubt. But it did not interest him anymore. She paid the price and deserved it. When the excitement died down, Ebony started to point out and explain the phone features to anyone who cared to listen, with her voice rising higher than usual.

Ejiofor also noticed that she dashed to the assembly ground with the phone, but on reaching there, she had to put it in her school bag to avoid getting punished by a school prefect.

When classes officially began for the day, Ejiofor could not stop throwing irritated glances in Ebony's direction—her getting a phone was not a problem but staying glued to it while a class was on, spoke badly of her senses.

Nnabugo walked in right after lunch break and Ejiofor had the answer to one of his numerous questions. Nnabugo kept his eyes on Ebony at the slightest opportunity he got. He would run his tongue over his lower lip and then turn back to face the chalkboard. Ebony boldly displayed the phone on her desk while she was on it and Nnabugo did not bother to say anything concerning that, instead, he punished a boy for whispering. Ejiofor was convinced beyond doubt that Ebony was now one of Nnabugo's preys.

It irked him to think that he once called her a good girl, showered praises on her and told her on countless occasions, that she was different from the other girls in school.

"Stop overthinking so you won't die young," Enyioma whispered to Ejiofor.

"I'm not overthinking," Ejiofor countered. "I'm just wondering how someone would open her eyes and decide to ruin her future because of temporary satisfaction."

"Stop wondering," Enyioma said, smiling. "The future will tell. Unfortunately, one unsuspecting and innocent man will marry her in the future."

Ejiofor shook his head. He did not know who the man would be, but he already felt sympathy towards him.

CHAPTER TWENTY

It was a sunny Saturday afternoon. Ebony sat in front of her friend's house, talking and laughing over their escapades. Her friend, Ijeoma, was the one she usually consulted whenever she thought something was starting to go wrong or whenever she needed any form of advice. It was Ijeoma who encouraged her to leave Davies for 'dulling her shine' and stick to Mr Nnabugo.

"Ijeoma!" A feminine voice called from the back of the house.

"Yes, mommy!" Ijeoma answered. She excused herself and left to meet her mother.

She returned a few minutes later and set down a plate of *abacha,* made by her mother. She went back to get a jug of water and two cups, before inviting Ebony to join her.

"Hmmm... if not for my lack of appetite, this *abacha* is actually delicious," Ebony said as she licked her lips after the first spoon. However, she could not ignore how Ijeoma stared at her. "Ijeoma, what is the matter? You've been looking at me suspiciously since I got here," she asked.

"Ebony, you're adding some weight, and… I noticed that you always sleep in class. I think I should be the one asking what the matter is. What is happening to you?"

"I don't know o. I am always very weak, even eating is now a problem. I get irritated by almost every food that comes my way," Ebony lamented.

"That's weird," Ijeoma stated. "When last did you see your period? You might be pregnant."

Ebony laughed. "How can I get pregnant? Me of all people getting pregnant. That's not possible. I always play it safe."

Ijeoma shook her head. "Anybody can make a mistake. Some preventive methods can fail. So tell me, when last did you see it?"

Ebony scratched her head. "I haven't seen it for a while, but it's nothing. It has happened to me before and it came back after three months."

"I think you are pregnant this time. Fatigue, food aversion, morning sickness and weight gain, Ebony you must be pregnant. No two ways about this."

Ebony shook her head. She knew Mr Nnabugo as an experienced man who would not make the mistake of getting her pregnant. He had assured her several times that a student getting pregnant for him was unheard of and that it would never happen.

Besides, she knew all there was to know about preventive measures, but, what if she was pregnant. Is the constant fatigue a part of pregnancy symptoms?

"Ebony, I think you should go and talk to him now," Ijeoma placed a hand on her shoulders. "He's older. If you are pregnant, he will find a solution before people get to know."

Ebony instantly became worried. From the way Ijeoma spoke, it seemed she was convinced about the pregnancy. She did not want to be pregnant, all she ever wanted was to get a mobile phone, and she now had it. She did not need any complications. Pregnancy was never part of her plans.

"Ijeoma, do you think I'm pregnant?" Ebony quavered.

Ijeoma smiled to ease the tension in the air. "You might not be pregnant, but if you are, he will find a solution. Stop panicking, you are not the first girl to get pregnant." Ijeoma's voice dropped low. "I have gotten pregnant before and nobody knew because I handled it well."

"You don't mean it?" Ebony's eyes widened in surprise.

"I'm serious," Ijeoma bragged. "If you are smart, nobody will ever find out. So, cheer up and let's eat. After that, you can go and talk to Mr Nnabugo."

Ebony nodded and scooped a portion of *abacha* from the plate. Ijeoma's confession gave her a level of confidence she never imagined she had. Whatever the outcome was, she was more than willing to face the consequences. One thing was sure; she was not ready to become a mother—not while she was still in class two or attracted so much attention from the men who came across her.

She finished and left for Mr Nnabugo's house. On her way there, she kept wondering how he would react to the news if eventually it was confirmed that she was pregnant. She had heard countless stories of men who denied having anything to do with a girl when they discovered that she was pregnant. She wondered what would happen if Nnabugo does something similar. Would the mobile phone be worth the humiliation she would experience if he did? She already had to go through experiences she never wanted, just to get the mobile phone. How would she cope with pregnancy?

No doubt, the news of her pregnancy would automatically bring an end to her schooling. Her parents would be disappointed in her, and her brothers would beat up Nnabugo. Despite the fact that he was her father's close friend, she always knew her brothers never liked him because of his bad reputation of womanizing.

The first day her brothers and parents found out about the phone she got from Nnabugo, her immediate elder brother had insisted she returned it. But she was able to convince her father that the phone would help her in school, especially with research and mathematics. Therefore, he let her keep it, but not without saying a big 'thank you' to his friend.

Ebony wanted the story to remain that way. She did not want her family to know about her relationship with her father's close friend; neither did she want a situation where they would force her to return the phone or drop out of school.

She reached Nnabugo's home at about 3:15 P.M and rapped her knuckle on the door.

"Who's there?" His voice came from within.

"It's Ebony. I came to see you."

She heard footsteps and in the next minute, the door gave way to reveal his elderly face with grey beard. He was a man in his mid-fifties with four children and two grandchildren, yet, he dressed and acted like he was in his early twenties. Despite his age, he was an attractive man; tall, dark and lanky. His features were part of what attracted Ebony to him.

"Baby girl," he danced back and forth like a playboy and Ebony smiled painfully. Then, he stepped aside to let her in. "I never knew I would see your beautiful face today. Smile for me, real smile."

Ebony managed a tight-lipped smile in his direction as she walked into the simply furnished sitting room to find textbooks around the place.

"You don't seem happy," he said, running a hand over her arms. "What's the problem?"

"I'm pregnant," Ebony wailed.

He stepped backwards and took a quick look over her body. "Why did you say so?"

"I have been sleeping and falling sick. Ijeoma thinks I'm pregnant and I think so too."

"Is that why you look worried? It's a minor issue. I will take you to a hospital on Monday. If you are pregnant, they will tell us, and we will do something about it. Now smile for me."

All of Ebony's earlier fears vanished into thin air and she smiled. She counted herself lucky that Nnabugo neither argued nor asked if he was responsible for the pregnancy. If he had, that would have been the genesis of her problems. Just like Ijeoma did, she would get rid of the pregnancy and move on with her life.

'So, that's how Nnabugo has been impregnating students and aborting it after all?' The thought made her shudder and she wrapped her hands over her arms.

She spent the rest of the day in his house and only left when it was dark. She knew her parents would ask questions if she did not get home on time.

On Monday morning, she was among the first set of students to show up in school. Showing up in time had become a habit since she no longer had to wait for Davies.

She managed to smile and laugh with other students as if all was well, but inwardly, she could not wait to accomplish her major plan for the day. As soon as the bell rang for lunch break, Ebony picked up her bag and left the school. Earlier on, Nnabugo had slipped a paper containing an address into her hands and outlined the necessary plans to her.

"Be there in time, let's find a solution before anyone finds out," he had repeated to her.

Ebony knew the place very well and she knew exactly what they do there, having heard from other girls, but she was not perturbed. She just needed a solution to the mess she was in and did not care what it would cost.

She got to the address and the first thing she noticed outside the building was Nnabugo's Suzuki motorcycle. She confidently walked in and found him sitting at the reception.

Nnabugo saw her and stood. "Thanks for coming on time. Let's get started."

Ebony nodded and looked around the clinic.

Nnabugo summoned the lady at the counter who walked over to meet him.

"This is the girl I told you about. If she's pregnant..."

"She's pregnant," the lady answered, looking closely at Ebony. "It's obvious to anyone who's observant."

"Then you know what to do," Nnabugo mumbled.

All through the conversation, Ebony stood, looking from Nnabugo to the woman. The experience was new to her and she could not think of anything to say. She only nodded when the lady asked that she follow her into the adjoining room.

In the room, she sat on a bed while the lady took out a bottle of liquid and a syringe. She drew the liquid into the syringe before turning to Ebony.

"I need you to trust me and calm down." She spoke while cleaning a part of her arm with a ball of alcohol-soaked cotton wool. "You won't feel a thing after this."

On a normal day, Ebony would have jumped at the sight of a needle, but this time, she was calm—all she wanted was an end to the process.

She winced when the needle pricked her skin. The lady asked her to lie on the bed and she immediately did as she was told. That was the last thing she remembered.

Chapter Twenty-One

When she opened her eyes, Ebony realized she was in the company of Nnabugo and the nurse. They were both seated at the other side of the room, opposite her. Her body felt weak, as though she had moved a truckload of cement while on the bed, but that was not her major concern, the process she had undergone was. Was it successful? If yes, why was she feeling so weak?

She recalled Ijeoma telling her that the process was simple, and she would wake up hale and hearty as though she had just gone to sleep. So why was she feeling different?

Ebony turned her head and tried to speak, but she felt the words trapped in her throat. She tried again yet got the same result. She did the only thing she could think of, she cried until she got someone's attention.

It worked! The nurse was the first to notice the tears, then she alerted Nnabugo, who also turned to stare at her with sympathy written all over his face.

Ebony wondered what was amiss. Why did they have such looks on their faces? Should they not be excited that the procedure was successful? Ebony's mind was in turmoil. She longed to ask those questions from the two people who had the answers, but the words dried up as soon as they reached her lips.

"Ebony, can you hear me? Are you okay?" The nurse inquired.

Ebony managed to move her head sideways in response to the question. She was nowhere near okay. She could barely move her body, but for the sake of her sanity, she had to pretend she was okay. Another panic-stricken expression from the nurse would have shattered her heart. Right there and then, she started to regret her actions. If she had not wanted a phone so badly, she would not have found herself in such an ugly situation. For the first time in her life, she realized why some people practised contentment as if their lives depended on it. She wished she was contented with what she had.

"Are you okay?" Nnabugo asked.

Ebony opened her mouth to speak again, and this time, the words came out. "I... feel very... weak."

"You will be fine," the nurse affirmed and then turned to Nnabugo. "I told you this was going to happen. She was four months gone already."

Nnabugo looked at Ebony and lowered his head.

"Am I going to be okay?" Ebony asked in tears.

The nurse placed a hand on her shoulder and smiled. "You will be fine. It will take a little more time than usual, but you will."

Ebony spent another thirty minutes in the small, ugly-looking room with worn out paints, before the nurse told Nnabugo that she was fit to leave. Unlike when she first woke up, she now felt her legs and could even walk some distance by herself.

With Nnabugo's help, Ebony walked to the door and got on his motorcycle. He hurried back in and spoke briefly with the nurse before he hurried out again.

"You will be fine," Nnabugo assured her for the umpteenth time.

Ebony nodded. She wished she could wholeheartedly believe him.

He took her back to school and stopped close to the school gates. The plan was for her to alight there to avoid further suspicions and talks amongst the students and even teachers. He rode in while Ebony slowly walked in and headed to her classroom.

Her classroom had a back door, which usually served as a quick entrance whenever a student was late. She walked in through the door and noticed Ijeoma giving her a curious stare. Ebony understood her silent question and answered with a nod, before taking her seat.

She felt too weak to listen to what Mrs Florence Urekan, the English teacher, was saying. Besides, her stomach and inner hip felt like a lit gas cooker. Mrs Florence was a huge dark woman with a punk hairstyle, and a face void of makeup. She rarely held a cane, but no teacher had the kind of force she applied while flogging, be it male or female teachers.

Ebony placed her head on her desk—not minding if she would get flogged—and dozed off. She did not know for how long she slept, but she woke up to the noise of her classmates. Weakly, she looked around, wondering what was going on, only to realize that the class was over, and all eyes were on her. She realized that they were staring at her skirt. She looked down at it and realized she was not only soaked but was sitting in a pool of her own blood.

Someone screamed and ran out to call the teachers while the others stared at her in fright. Fear gripped Ebony. Was she dying or what? Would she ever make it out of this mess? What would the teachers say?

What would they tell her parents? She stood to run away from the classroom, but she only took two steps before she collapsed and passed out.

When she opened her eyes, she was lying on a bed in a much cleaner room than the previous one. She briefly wondered where she was, but it did not take long before she found out. The drip fixed to her hand was a good piece of evidence. She was in the health centre which was a few miles away from her school.

Ebony was wondering who brought her there when the door opened and a nurse walked in, smiling.

"How are you feeling now?"

"I'm fine," Ebony answered.

The nurse nodded and moved to carry out her routine check.

Ebony honestly thought she felt better than she had since she woke up at the other nurse's place. She was no longer weak; the burning sensation had disappeared, and she no longer felt dizzy. All parts of her body felt normal, although her conscience smote her. She deeply regretted her actions.

With what happened in class, she knew she was already the topic of discussion for every student in school. The rumour she was trying to avoid was going to spread in a much bitter and sorrowful way. Everyone who saw it was definitely going to concoct stories just to paint her darker than she already was.

The nurse finished checking her vital signs and turned to her. "Your English teacher rushed you in with the help of one other teacher. We thought you would not make it. Tell me, who did this to you?"

Ebony could not answer the question; instead, she started to cry. How would she explain the kind of mess she had put herself in?

The nurse sat on the bed and held Ebony's hand. "I'll advise you to say the truth so that we can help you. You are lucky you survived this, and we are willing to help you feel better."

"The lady said I was four months gone and that was why she encountered some complications," Ebony confessed.

The door creaked open and Mrs Florence strolled in.

"Ebony, how are you feeling?"

Ebony nodded. "I'm fine. Thank you for your help, ma."

Ebony could not thank her enough for her help and for not criticizing her. Even though she could see the disappointment on the elderly woman's face, she was glad the woman still smiled at her.

"What happened to you?" Mrs Florence queried, sitting at the edge of the bed. Her huge weight depressed the bed.

Ebony remembered the nurse's words and truthfully narrated her experience to both women.

"The deed has been done, but you young girls live too carelessly, I must say," the nurse spoke after Ebony was done with her narration.

"I wish I didn't do it," Ebony sobbed.

The nurse turned to Mrs Florence and mumbled with pity. "Her womb was damaged during the procedure."

Ebony looked up at the nurse, hoping to hear that it was a prank, but the nurse had a look on her face that showed she was serious about what she said.

"I'm sorry," she muttered to Ebony.

The ocean of tears she never thought she had flowed down her cheeks. A damaged womb meant that she would never get pregnant again nor have her own child. *'God, what did I put myself into?'* Ebony lamented silently.

CHAPTER TWENTY-TWO

Mrs Florence faintly smiled at Ebony. "I will ask a student who knows your house to go and call your parents. Is that fine by you?"

Ebony nodded at Mrs Florence. She had reached that point where being secretive was no longer an option. Her secrets were out; the nurses in the hospital and Mrs Florence knew them.

"I will be right back," Mrs Florence said and walked out.

Ebony turned her face to the wall as tears trickled down her cheeks. How did life become this unfair to her? She knew how much she had ignored the warnings of her parents and brothers to stay away from having affairs with men, and she understood how disappointed they would be when news of her ordeal gets to them. All she had now were regrets and disappointments.

If she could rewind time, she would stay away from every man and just focus on the main reason she was in school, to study and become a lawyer. She would not allow her beauty or whistles and talks from boys get to her head.

She heaved. If wishes were horses, beggars would probably eat the best meals.

Ebony did not know for how long she stayed in that position, brooding and lamenting, but she heard the door open. She did not turn around because she was too sad and emotionally down to worry about who walked in. She felt a gentle pat on her back and turned to see who it was. It was Ijeoma. She had the soberest expression on her face.

"Ebony, how are you feeling?"

That was it. Ebony let loose the tears she had been holding back.

Ijeoma stepped closer, draped an arm over Ebony's body and whispered into her ear, "You will be fine. Please stop crying."

Ebony wished it was that easy to stop crying, nonetheless, she put in efforts to stop. When she finally did, a series of sniffs followed. She looked up at Ijeoma and the questions in her friend's eyes were as clear as crystal.

"My womb was damaged in the process."

Ijeoma's eyes widened in shock and she covered her mouth with her hands. "How? Why? Mine went very smoothly."

Ebony shrugged. *'I'm the unlucky one, I guess.'*

Ebony was about to say something when her mother walked into the room, her eyes red with anger. She was an epitome of beauty from where Ebony got hers. Fair, tall and slender.

"Ebony Ozoemena, you see what you've done to yourself? You see?" Her mother screamed at her. "Stay one place, you won't listen. Are you happy now?"

"I'm sorry, mother," Ebony pleaded amidst fresh tears. "It was not intentional."

Her mother stared at her, shaking her head. "Whatever you sow, you will reap. You will face the consequences of your actions, not me. I brought you up the way a mother should. Have I ever maltreated you?"

Ebony shook her head in response.

"Good. Ebony, do you know how many times I have denied myself some necessities just so I could provide and buy you the things you deserve as my first daughter?" Mrs Ozoemena wailed.

The door opened again. It was Mrs Florence and the nurse.

"You are here," the English teacher said, looking at Mrs Ozoemena. "That was fast."

Ebony watched her mother break down in tears instead of replying the teacher. It shattered her heart to know that her carelessness was the sole cause of her mother's sadness.

All she ever wanted was to study hard, become successful and live the best life. She knew how much her mother, who was only a schoolteacher, had sacrificed for her. Ebony wore some of the best clothes among her peers even though they were not short and flashy like she wanted. Since both her parents were teachers and were always owed salaries, she knew how many times her parents had borrowed money so they could feed well.

"Mommy please, I'm sorry for what I've done," Ebony cried and begged her mother.

The nurse shook her head at the scene. "I wish you kids would think about the attendant consequences before involving yourselves in things. See what you're doing to your mother."

"Ebony, who did this to you?" her mother asked, staring at her with tear-filled eyes.

The nurse hurried to Mrs Ozoemena and held her hand. "Please sit, ma, before we talk about this."

Mrs Ozoemena obliged and sat on the chair next to the bed before turning to Ebony for explanations.

"It's the maths teacher in her school," the nurse announced when Ebony said nothing.

Mrs Ozoemena's mouth dropped open. "Yo…ur… your teacher? Mr Nnabugo?"

Ebony nodded.

"Hei!" Mrs Ozoemena held her head with both hands. "This child you have killed me o! You have killed me. Mr Nnabugo? The same Nnabugo?"

"Do you know him?" The nurse asked.

"He is my husband's friend. *Chai!*"

The nurse's hand went to her mouth and she shook her head while staring at Ebony.

"He bought a phone for her, I said nothing because I didn't think he was a bad person. I trusted him; my husband trusted him." She turned to Ebony. "I trusted you too. I'm terribly disappointed in you. I'm going to your school right now!" She stood up and adjusted her wrapper, but Mrs Florence held her back.

"First, school is closed for today. Second, you are too angry to confront the man. You need to calm your nerves; the deed has been done and getting angry is not going to do anyone any good."

At about 7:15 P.M. when her mother asked the nurse if her daughter was fit to go home and she responded positively, Ebony was not pleased with the news. She wished she never woke up from the abortion bed. In fact, all she wanted was to remain in the comfort of the hospital room, away from the outside world. There was also her father and brothers to worry about. However, she had to face the consequences of her actions.

When they got home that evening, her mother narrated Ebony's ordeal to the family and all hell broke loose.

Her father yelled at her and seized the phone, while her four brothers each picked up a cutlass or stick and ran into the night. Ebony knew they were going to Nnabugo's house.

The boys soon returned; angry they did not meet Nnabugo at home. Of course, they turned their anger on Ebony. It took lots of pleading from their mother before they allowed her to go to bed.

The next morning, her parents stormed the school compound; disrupting the morning assembly. They were accompanied by Ebony and her four brothers who all wielded different sizes of machetes.

On their way there, Ebony had tried to plead with them to exercise a little patience, so they could go in when the assembly was over. Unfortunately, her pleas only caused them to hasten their steps.

"Every day is for the thief, but one day, the owner of the chicken will have his own say. Do you think I'm happy with you? I am ashamed of you. I am ashamed to call you my daughter!" Mr Ozoemena wailed.

In the end, they left Ebony no choice but to follow them.

"Where's Nnabugo?" her mother shouted. "Where's that man who doesn't know that he's old enough to zip up?"

"If you people don't produce him, we will destroy this school!" Her father threatened.

Murmurs started amongst the students as they turned their focus on Mr and Mrs Ozoemena. Ebony bowed her head, wishing she could vanish into thin air. She was having a double dose of embarrassment in two days. Her brothers were not helping matters as they kept destroying the flowers around the assembly ground with their machetes.

The headteacher walked to them and tried to hold Mrs Ozoemena, but she pushed her hand away. "Where's Mr Nnabugo? He's the one we came for. Teachers are supposed to guide their students, not mess up their lives, get them pregnant and destroy their wombs."

At the mention of wombs, the murmuring increased among the students, some of them had even started to laugh.

Mrs Florence came forward. "Ma, we are deeply saddened by what happened and Mr Nnabugo has a lot of questions to answer, but first, you have to calm..."

"See him, see him!" The students' voices interrupted Mrs Florence's plea. They screamed excitedly while pointing in the direction of Mr Nnabugo.

Ebony looked in the direction of their fingers and saw Mr Nnabugo at the far left of the school building with another teacher, obviously running from her parents. Mr Nnabugo had promised her that he would stick with her no matter what happened, yet, there he was, trying to escape. She felt silly for believing his words.

Mr Ozoemena went after Mr Nnabugo with his glistening machete, but some male teachers held him back. However, his sons moved swiftly and caught up with the man. While the other teacher tried to calm them down and insist that it was best to get the offender to the police station, the eldest of the boys cleared Nnabugo off his feet and descended on him with blows and cuts.

As soon as Mr Ozoemena was able to free himself from the hold of the teachers, he and his wife joined their sons. Some of the other teachers had to join them, pleading that jungle justice was not the way to go.

The excited students who were enjoying the scene booed and screamed Mr Nnabugo's name at the top of their voices. They continued booing Mr Nnabugo until some of the teachers whisked him away through the back gate to the police station.

As Ebony went with them, she realized that back in the school compound; she could not look any of the students in the face, including Ejiofor. Worse, she heard the murmurs and snide remarks directed at her.

She had not fully recovered from the ordeal at the abortion centre, but she was completely disappointed in herself. If she had stayed true to the plans she made when she first walked into the school, she would be in her uniform at the assembly ground, not dressed in casual wear with angry parents and brothers bearing machetes.

CHAPTER TWENTY-THREE

After the ugly scene witnessed right on the assembly ground, Ejiofor's countenance changed. Ebony had looked so pale and unkempt in less than twenty-four hours since he had seen her in a pool of her own blood. He felt sympathy towards her. The beauty he used to admire was still there, but faint. He wished he could turn back the hands of time and put more effort into talking Ebony out of her wayward ways. He sincerely wished she had paid more attention to her books and future than her looks and material things.

Now that everything was out in the open, Ejiofor realized that Mr Nnabugo was the one who got her the phone and got her pregnant. He could not argue with the fact that it was probably a trade by barter sort of transaction, but he was disappointed that Ebony could go that low just to get a phone.

He was still deep in thoughts when Enyioma wandered into the class and sat beside him. "Your former girlfriend is in trouble. She has ruined her life because of one small thing that will probably not exist in the next ten years."

Ejiofor rolled his eyes at him. "She was never my girlfriend; we were just good friends."

"Just good friends? And you kept dreaming of marrying her in the future?" Enyioma teased, lightly punching Ejiofor's shoulders.

"What is it? Why do you have that smile on your face?" Ejiofor asked, ignoring the sarcasm in his voice.

"I'm just coming from the staff room. The teachers were all talking about Ebony." Enyioma informed him. "Turns out she had an abortion."

Ejiofor's mouth opened wide. "Wow! That explains yesterday's issue of blood."

"Exactly," Enyioma answered excitedly. "Mr Nnabugo took her to a nurse who did a quack abortion on her, that's why she started bleeding."

Ejiofor shook his head. "Ebony doesn't deserve this, all she wanted was a phone."

True, they were no longer friends, but he still had some atom of sympathy and humanity left in him. The images of the 'innocent' Ebony he used to know flashed through his mind. He recalled the way she smiled, threw her head back when she laughed and how she always teased him about one thing or another. He felt terribly sad for her.

He recalled a time during lunch break when they were behind the canteen and a group of girls sitting beside them gossiped another girl who had an abortion. Ebony had expressed how outright disgusted she was by the act and immediately condemned it. Ejiofor wished she had kept to those words, belief, and standard.

"I don't know o," Enyioma said, interrupting Ejiofor's thoughts, "but I think I heard someone say that the abortion damaged her womb and she would never be able to give birth."

Ejiofor hissed. "You all should stop adding pepper and salt to whatever story you hear just to spice it and make it sound better.

Didn't you see Ebony this morning? Did she look like someone without a womb?"

Enyioma smiled. "Same way you can't tell a woman's age by looking at her, you can't also tell who has a womb and who doesn't. I strongly believe it is true. If it is a quack nurse like they said, then I'm sure they must have used one of those abortion instruments of theirs to damage her womb."

"You sound like you've done it before."

It was Enyioma's turn to hiss at the silly talk. "I read virtually anything that comes my way, especially medical stuff and I have read about the procedure before. Trust me, from what I read in those articles, if you pay me to undergo such a procedure, I will not even look at the money, let alone do the job. It's the most nauseating thing in the universe." Enyioma said, and feigned puke.

"Are you sure you'll be able to study medicine and surgery? When you finish pretending to vomit, bring out your English studies notebook because Mrs Florence is here," Ejiofor announced, pointing at the window.

Seconds later, the teacher walked in and they all stood to greet her.

"Sit," she ordered.

They did as told, and she started the lesson for the day. Halfway into the class, two girls giggled aloud as they gossiped.

Mrs Florence asked them to stand. "What's making you girls laugh?"

"We are sorry, ma," they answered in unison.

"This is how it starts, giggling and gossiping in class so the teachers will notice you. That's why you girls keep falling into the wrong hands. Imagine if you had kept quiet and listened like everyone else, would I notice you or call you out?"

They both shook their heads in response.

"Caution yourselves o," Mrs Florence said, wagging a finger at them and the rest of the class. "Students, listen. You all know Ebony, your classmate. And you all saw what happened in class yesterday and at the assembly ground today. Henceforth, I want you all to be careful with the way you live your lives. There's always a consequence for every action. Even if the consequence doesn't come now like Ebony's, it might come later in future. Live a good life and you will also reap its fruit."

A murmur arose from the students, while Ejiofor placed a hand on his chest, listening.

The teacher walked to the centre of the classroom and stood still, looking from one student to the other. "For you girls in this class, any teacher or male student who starts telling you how much they love you and how they will marry you in future, are your enemies. You are still young and have your whole life ahead of you. If you finish here, there is senior secondary school, and then there is the university, waiting for you. You will meet a lot of people at the university, and since you will be older or wiser, you will make rational decisions. For now, focus on your studies and ignore anybody telling you that they love you. The truth is, they don't. Just look at Ebony and how she ruined her life with her two hands, all because of a phone."

The murmuring became louder and the teacher held up her hand to get them to keep quiet.

Ejiofor shook his head. *'I warned her! If only she had listened to me, she wouldn't be the subject of today's sermon.'*

He turned to her seat and his eyes met with Ijeoma's. His frown deepened. He knew Ijeoma to be the ringleader of Ebony's squad, but there she was, acting so innocent.

"As for Ebony, she lived a very rough life and the price was her womb," Mrs Florence announced, strolling back to the front desk to pick up her lesson note.

"Her womb?" One of the female students asked, unable to hold back her curiosity.

The teacher turned; her lips straightened into a thin line. "Yes, her womb. The abortion damaged her womb and she will never be able to give birth again. Listen, boys and girls, if you like do not live a good life, such bad things happen."

The bell marking the end of the period sounded. As soon as the teacher left, the classroom became rowdy with discussions of Ebony.

Enyioma turned to Ejiofor with a look that said, 'I told you.' Ejiofor turned the other way, ignoring him. He was deeply saddened by what he just heard. For the want of a phone, Ebony lost her precious womb. He had once imagined Ebony giving birth to beautiful kids who looked just like her. So, all of that was never going to happen?

He knew she was going to face the consequences of her actions, but he did not know it was going to be this enormous. "I guess everyone should mind the way they live because some consequences are too dire to bear," Ejiofor murmured.

CHAPTER TWENTY-FOUR

After the shocking revelations, everyone in the room had their jaws hanging low except for Ebony who was in tears. Ejiofor had a mischievous smirk plastered on his face.

Ebony sniffled amidst the downpour of tears. She remembered staying home for one month right after the abortion. Her parents had vowed not to spend another dime on her in the name of schooling. After persistent pleas from her and Mrs Florence, who had taken her to the health centre, her father's heart finally melted and she continued schooling but not in the same school. Her father got a transfer and took her to the new school where he was teaching.

In the new environment, she understood that she had been schooling in paradise. Her father practically restricted her movement, kept her under close watch and made sure that she never mingled with any of the male students in her class. He had students watching her every move and she did not dare speak to a male student.

She did not dare go close to the staff room, not to mention laughing with any male teacher. She could not blame her father for all those restrictions; she was reaping the fruit of her waywardness.

Ebony cried louder. She regretted the day she got involved with Davies, she wished she could take back the day Mr Nnabugo caught them at the farm, she wished she had declined his offer and just cancelled the thought of having a mobile phone.

"Is it true you can't give birth? Like ever, in your life?" Ekwueme asked with doubt, staring down at where she knelt.

Ebony nodded slowly. "That's what the nurse said, but I don't know if it's true."

Senator Adams hissed and shook his head. "Young girls, young people... see, I really don't know how long it will take for you people to learn that everything you do in life comes with its own reward. Why choose to do the bad, when you can do good and reap the fruit thereof? See what you caused yourself. Whatever phone you wanted then has probably gone into extinction like three or five years ago but see what it caused you. Material things don't last."

He turned to Ekwueme. "You need to see what university girls are doing nowadays, following politicians old enough to be their grandfathers. When I see young girls doing all manner of things to get the latest iPhone, I always shake my head at such foolishness. All those things will soon fade away; new and better ones will replace them. What will they do to get the new ones then?"

"It's a pity that our youths and teenagers no longer think of the future. Do they think they will remain at that age forever? They're going to grow and start regretting all those things while blaming village people or witches for their predicament." Senator Ezeuwa chipped in; his arms crossing his chest.

"I'm more bothered about the fact that she led me on without letting the cat out of the bag until Ejiofor showed up. She let me do the introduction without any form of remorse. You all should have seen how excited she was on that day, happy that she finally found someone she would string along with her problematic life."

"If I had told you, I know you would have hated me," Ebony muttered amidst tears.

Ekwueme shook his head. "Why would I hate you? It's your life, and I have no right to judge you and tell you how you should live. Certainly, I have no right to hate you over how you choose to live, but I sincerely wish you had thought about the future while doing all of that."

"I was too naive."

"You were old enough to make your decisions," Ejiofor shot back at her. "I warned you. I talked to you several times and asked you to change your ways and the kind of company you kept, but you played deaf to my words. Your crime would have been less had you not tried to poison me too."

Ebony turned to Ejiofor, "I am sorry. I am sincerely sorry."

"It's too late now," Ejiofor smiled at her in displeasure. "I am sure you will get married, but not to my brother."

Senator Adams waved his hand at Ejiofor. "It is obvious your brother fell in love with her, and her past is past. I think the most important thing we should do now is let him make his decision. The wedding cards are out, the Porsche car which your brother bought for her as a wedding gift is parked in the garage—well decorated, and the news of their upcoming wedding is spreading."

Senator Ekwueme sighed in frustration. "I have never been this confused in my life. I truly loved her, but I don't know if I still do. It is somewhat painful to think that she not only tried to poison my brother, she also didn't trust me enough to share this with me before the relationship progressed to this level. If Ejiofor had not come around, she would have kept smiling with me while I talked about babies and family until we got to the altar. Then three or four months later, she would start shedding crocodile tears and telling me that she forgot to mention her past, or maybe even pretend like she didn't know she could not have a child."

Senator Adams turned to Ebony. "See how you people lose good men because of carelessness and mistakes. Are you sure you can't have your own child?"

Ebony nodded. "That's what the nurse told me."

"Have you carried out any other test on yourself?" Senator Adams queried.

She shook her head. "I have never bothered to confirm if she lied or said the truth."

Senator Adams got off his seat, walked to Ekwueme, and placed a hand on his shoulders. "I think the best thing to do now is to find out if you can both have a child before you take any decision. It's not every day we find someone we genuinely love. Let's not allow her mistakes to ruin everything you share. Growing up, I knew what I wanted to be today. I know things I avoided, so that nothing ruins plans for me. I sincerely wished she had done the same, but since she didn't, let's forge ahead. We can't keep crying over spilled milk."

"While we ponder on what to do about her almost poisoning your brother, I think you should go to the hospital and confirm the womb part of the story. It's important," Senator Takwas added.

"You are right," Ekwueme sighed, getting to his feet. "Let's go to my doctor's, Miss Ebony."

Hearing him call her first name caused Ebony's tears to flow more. He had never addressed her by that title before. Not even the day they met. With tears in her eyes, she rose and followed him outside.

Ekwueme beckoned Philip, his personal assistant, to drive them to the hospital. Philip got the car ready and the duo stepped in. On the drive to the hospital, Ekwueme refused to look at Ebony, neither did he permit physical contact.

The hospital was only ten minutes' drive away from the mansion; it did not take long to get there. Ekwueme had already made calls while they were in the car, so his doctor was waiting when they walked into the hospital.

Ekwueme narrated the issue on ground to his doctor and requested a referral to a female doctor who would examine Ebony. The doctor nodded, strolled out and came back a few minutes later with a lady, probably in her late forties.

She exchanged pleasantries with Ekwueme and turned to Ebony. "Let's go to my office, madam."

Ebony stood to follow her.

Ekwueme made to go with them, but the doctor shook her head at him. "Please wait here, sir. She will be right back."

Ebony followed the doctor to a private office and the examination started. Thirty minutes later, the doctor stared Ebony in the eye. "Let me guess, it was a quack abortion?"

Ebony nodded and tears dripped down her cheeks. She knew she had done more harm to herself than good and she knew her fate already.

"Do you want me to tell him, or you will?" the doctor asked, putting away her instruments.

"Please go ahead and tell him," Ebony answered. She knew she would never be able to look Ekwueme in the face, not to mention telling him something as heavy as that.

"It's not the end of the world, you know," the doctor asserted, consoling Ebony.

Ebony shook her head. She knew it was the end of her own world with Ekwueme. She went with the doctor to the office where Ekwueme sat, and the doctor broke the news to him.

Chapter Twenty-Five

The news the doctor shared with Ekwueme pierced his heart. He tried to look at Ebony, but the weight of the news made his head too heavy to move. How she managed to look so innocent and fool him until Ejiofor showed up still baffled him.

"Doctor, are you sure it's no longer there?"

"I am very sure of the result. It's hundred percent accurate."

"Thank you." Ekwueme greeted both doctors, and walked out.

He was too angry to utter a word to anyone as he and Ebony scurried out of the hospital. He did not even halt to exchange pleasantries with a woman who tried getting his attention by chanting, 'Senator, senator, good afternoon, sir!'

He marched to the car, slid in, and sat quietly. The driver turned and tried to speak to him, but Ekwueme held up a hand, waving him to silence. Ebony walked out of the hospital, crying profusely. The driver opened the car door and she stepped in.

Ekwueme hissed at the sight of her. She tried to talk, but he silenced her with a wave of the hand. He was too pained to talk to her. She betrayed him, betrayed his trust for her and worst of all, she kept secrets.

Ekwueme remembered baring his all to her just before the introduction and even asked her to do the same. She had plainly told him that she did not have any skeleton in her cupboard. He did not know he was dining with a little demon who would try to poison his brother just to cover her secret.

He imagined what would have happened if she had succeeded. Ejiofor would die, he would mourn him and proceed with his marriage plans without suspecting that she masterminded the death. From all the things he had witnessed, he knew that lying or even going as far as killing to cover up one's secret, would lead to more killings, as the murderer would also have to take out the next set of persons who dared to unravel these secrets.

If she had mentioned her inability to bear a child to him earlier, he would have halted the marriage plans while they sought for a solution, but with everything she had done, there was no point keeping such an untrustworthy person in his life. He was better off without her.

The short drive back home was very uneventful, and when they reached the mansion, Ekwueme alighted before the driver could even find a proper parking space for the Range Rover. He stormed into the sitting room and all eyes turned to him. He knew they were waiting to hear the answers to the questions burning in their hearts.

"It's done," Ekwueme revealed, shrugging. "She can't have a child. The doctor confirmed it." He explained as he ran a hand over his face and dropped heavily in the nearest armchair.

"Are there alternatives you could easily opt for?" Senator Adams asked.

"I don't want to think about alternatives right now. I just need to put an end to all of this," Ekwueme replied, shaking his head.

"Sir, if you ask me, I would say you should send her packing right now," Ejiofor suggested. "She doesn't deserve you and also, she doesn't deserve a place in our family."

Senator Adams shook his head at Ejiofor. "Young people nowadays are actually hot-tempered; life doesn't work that way. If you ask me, I would say you are still harbouring some form of hatred towards her, you need to let go of that, it's not worth it."

Ejiofor shrugged without responding.

The door opened and Ebony walked in; tears smearing her face. They all turned to her and she curtsied without looking anyone in the eye. Sniffing, she staggered to Ekwueme and immediately knelt before him. "I am so sorry," she said and tried to hold his legs.

"Don't touch me!" he yelled.

Ebony turned to Ejiofor, "I am sincerely sorry for attempting to poison you. I was utterly desperate to cover my secrets, forgetting that there's nothing hidden under the sun that would not be uncovered. Please forgive me."

"I have nothing against you. The issue is now between you and my brother, my work here is done," Ejiofor responded, raising both hands to emphasize his point.

Ebony nodded and turned to senator Ekwueme. "God knows I am truly sorry, and I regret every bit of my actions, please forgive me this last time. I promise to live a better life. Please."

Ekwueme looked at her in amazement. "What gave you the effrontery to think of poisoning my younger brother? Don't blame it on your being desperate. I have been desperate a few times, and I have never attempted to kill anyone. I mean, how did you come up with such a wicked idea?"

"It will never happen again, I promise. I have learnt my lesson." Ebony pleaded as more tears flowed down her cheeks.

Ekwueme managed a painful smile as he looked down at her. "Again? There will never be a recurrence of what happened today. After all you have done, do you still expect me to go ahead with the marriage plans? Come on, grow up!"

Ebony held her head with both hands and almost fell to the floor, but one of the senators who was closest to her moved just in time to catch her.

She wriggled out of his grasp, threw herself before Ekwueme, and grabbed his legs. "I'm sorry, please," she begged, crying.

"This is not about being sorry, Ebony. I can't live with someone who is capable of thinking about murder, and not just that, you even acted on your thoughts. Again, I want children. I would really love to carry my own babies. There's no point going ahead with the marriage plans if you can't give me kids. I'm sorry too."

"We can do something about it," Ebony said.

"Do what?" Ekwueme bellowed at her. "There's nothing we can do here. I am just glad that Ejiofor exposed all of these before the wedding, if he didn't, I am quite sure you would never open up to me no matter how many years we stay trying to have a child."

"I think you should think this through before you make your decision." Senator Adams spoke to Ekwueme. "This is not the best time to make a decision; you are saying a lot of things in anger."

Ekwueme vigorously shook his head at him. "There's no need to wait. I am not judging her past, but I can't be in her future, that's all I am saying. I want kids, a lot of kids, and she obviously can't give me any. Is there any point sticking around?"

It was a while later Ekwueme observed that Ebony had become calm and composed. She wiped her tears and turned to face Ekwueme. "I am sorry for putting you through all of this, but it's okay. I accept my fate. I ruined my life with my own hands, and I must face the consequences. All I wish is that you would consider the love we once shared."

"Love can't conquer this. You've destroyed too much already; the love I had for you, your reputation, and every bit of trust I once had in you. I am sorry. I must call off the wedding and put an end to every preparation. I hope you find someone who is willing to accept you the way you are. I will need you to start packing your things, feel free to keep whatever gifts I've given you."

It hurt Ekwueme to say those words, but he knew he had to. He had always wanted kids and there was no way he would go ahead to marry a woman who could not give birth. He could not bring himself to trust her, after what she wanted to do to Ejiofor. Thank heavens Ejiofor was smart enough to figure out what she was up to. If not, he would never have known the kind of person he was about to marry.

He looked up at Senator Adams and the others, "I guess the whole reason for which you are here has crumbled. Don't give me that look of sympathy, I am fine."

CHAPTER TWENTY-SIX

Ebony strolled to the bedroom in tears. She looked around the vast and luxurious room and knew she was going to miss it. Before the bedroom was furnished, Ekwueme had asked her to pick the colours she liked most for the beddings, decor and other items since she was going to be spending a lot of her time there. She had gladly obliged as the dutiful wife-to-be. Little did she know that her past was going to bring about her ruin.

Her eyes rested on the portraits by each side of the wall; they were of a mother and a child in two different postures, and she had picked those for the room too.

Fresh tears trickled down her cheeks. She blamed herself for getting carried away by material things. She wished she had remembered that there was something called 'future' while she was living carelessly in secondary school; it would have helped her live a better life.

It was sad to think that the phone for which she had lost her womb was no longer in use. She looked at the phone she now had lying on the table. It was a hundred times better in value and beauty than the one she lost everything for.

If only she knew that a good name was better than gold and silver, she would have strived to make a good name for herself. Unfortunately, her bad choices in life just cost an excellent opportunity to marry the Senate President and live the kind of life she had always wanted. She knew a lot of girls who envied her during her introduction, and some who openly told her that they wished they were in her shoes. How would she face them now? How would she tell them that she destroyed the good thing that God put in her hands?

If she had known, she would have listened to Ejiofor back then when he used to advise her to live a good life. Well, she had thought that since she was beautiful and commanded more attention than he did, she was always going to be on top and there was no way she would cross paths with him in future, not to mention needing his help.

"See what I've done to myself!" Ebony sobbed, looking at her reflection in the floor-length mirror. "Had I known, I would have listened to all the good advice and lived a better life. I would not have kept the kind of company I did. I would not have been involved with Davies and Mr Nnabugo."

The people who helped her ruin her life were all living fine, but she was weeping and carrying her cross. *'Indeed, bad company corrupts good manners.'* Ebony thought and sighed.

She remembered the girls she mingled with in class. They were the ones who pushed her into doing all sorts of things just so she could get her own phone and bring it to school so that all of them would share. Had she known that none of them meant well for her, she would have distanced herself from them.

The last time she checked, Ijeoma was married with a daughter, and Davies was schooling abroad. Mr Nnabugo was alive and kicking. His kids were taking care of him. She was the only one paying for yesterday's mistakes in a terrible way.

"He ruined my life," Ebony covered her face with both hands. "He has kids and I will never be able to have mine."

She remembered all of her mother's advice regarding the opposite gender and love for material things, she wished she had adhered to all of them.

Her eyes went to a large photograph on the wall, directly above the edge of the bed. The picture was taken on the day of the introduction. Ekwueme had pointed out how she looked so beautiful in it and in the end, they had both decided to get it enlarged and framed.

She recalled that they had already made plans on where they were going to hang their wedding photos. Heck, she already had her wedding gown and traditional attire in the wardrobe. Her visa for a trip to the Caribbean was almost ready.

She made to open the box, which contained the wedding gown, but quickly decided it was best to let it be, seeing it would make her hate herself more.

Now that her secret was out, Ebony wished she had kept the pregnancy. The story would have been that she had a child. Unfortunately, all she had left were wishes upon wishes. She wished she had listened to reason and thought about the future, if she had, she would not have found herself in such a mess.

On second thoughts, Ebony opened the box and took out the wedding gown. She held it close to her bosom, sat on the floor, and gave in to heart-wrenching sobs. Without being told, she knew she had done a lot of damage to herself. Which man would think of marrying a lady without a womb?

She heard footsteps approaching from the passage. She quickly wiped her tears and began packing her bags.

Seconds later, Ekwueme walked in and stood next to her. She looked up at the handsome man she had fallen in love with and did not miss the sadness in his eyes.

"Ebony, I'm sorry that things had to end this way," Ekwueme started. "I really liked you and I wanted you in my life as my wife and partner, but you went too far by attempting to kill my brother. You could have come to me and talked to me about it. I can never bring myself to trust someone who could go as far as plotting murder just to cover one secret. If you had ten secrets, you would have made plans to kill ten people as well."

Ebony shook her head and looked away. She was ashamed of all she had done and the last thing she wanted to do was see more of the pained expression she knew she put on his face. She remembered the times he professed love to her and how he had made it known that he did not need another woman by his side except her. Now all of that had changed.

"It is fine," Ebony sniffed. "I understand. I'm sorry for hurting you in this manner. I could have told you when we first met."

"Yes, you should have told me," Ekwueme answered, his voice rising higher than it usually was. "The decision to either carry on or end the relationship would have been on me. What you did was deceitful and uncalled for. Were you thinking I was never going to find out?"

Ebony lowered her head and continued packing her clothes into her bag. She could not give Ekwueme the answer to that question. Yes, she knew he was going to find out, but she thought they would have been far gone—probably one or two years into the marriage.

When they first met, she did not know he was Ejiofor's elder brother. She remembered Ejiofor telling her that he had an elder brother in the city, but she never got to meet him before they parted ways. When Ekwueme approached her for marriage, she did notice the surname, but she thought it was a coincidence.

Again, Ekwueme never said anything about a younger brother until after they concluded their introduction. If she had not heard him lamenting about his brother's inability to show up because he travelled to the UK for a training as he had been appointed the Deputy Governor of the Central Bank, she would not have found out it was the same small Ejiofor she went to school with.

When she finally found out, she prayed hard for Ejiofor not to appear until after the wedding. Too bad that prayer came back to her unanswered.

"I wish you the best in life, Ebony. Hopefully, you'll find a good path." Ekwueme muttered and made for the door.

Ebony cried as she watched him leave. She did not need his wishes; he was all she wanted in her life. Now that she could never be with him, she was certain that she would never find the best again.

Chapter Twenty-Seven

Seven years later, nothing was the same. Ebony sat in a corner of a well-furnished bedroom, wiping her tears.

For the tenth time in two hours, she thought about the kind of life she ought to be living if only she had not made a terrible decision to pursue material things instead of her future goals and ambitions.

The last time she checked, Ekwueme was in his second tenure as the Senate President of the country, living fine with his wife and son. He had gotten married two years after their separation.

Regarding their separation, he had taken the blame for the failed relationship and kept reporters out of her way. Every morning after their separation, Ebony prayed and cried out to God that she wanted to wake up from her bad dream and go back to Ekwueme, but in the end, she had to face the reality and accept that they were never going to be together.

She reached for her phone and looked at the photos on display. Her tears doubled. On the screen was a picture of Ekwueme, his beautiful wife and son, enjoying the summer holiday in Paris.

"This would have been me," she cried out.

She did not care if her husband was in the living room or not. Right from the beginning, she had made it known to him that she still longed for Ekwueme. Her career as a lawyer would have skyrocketed. She would have loved and been loved.

Even with the huge societal wedding Ekwueme had, Ebony still found it difficult to come to terms with the fact that he had moved on and would never be her husband.

She had almost run mad when the news of their breakup got to the press. She saw her photos all over the internet and lots of people had varying opinions regarding the news. Some speculated that their genotype was not a match; some said that Ekwueme did not want a wife from his village and that explained the hasty breakup. Ebony knew the truth but could not tell anyone except her parents and siblings. She was, however, glad about the way Ekwueme handled the whole thing by taking the blame and not exposing her secrets to the whole country.

On several occasions, Ekwueme had organized programmes to advise youths and enlighten them on the dangers of some of the bad habits they practised. He would always end with the quote, 'While enjoying your youth, always remember that there's a place called future and what happens there directly depends on what you do today.'

The youths would clap and cheer him on, and Ebony would be in front of the television praying for them to adhere to the counsel, not because it was the Senate President speaking but because it was the truth of life. If she had listened when someone gave her that piece of advice, she would have been living in a mansion in Abuja and not a three-bedroom apartment in Lagos with a sixty-year-old grandpa whose children were much older than she was. How she ended up with a sixty-year-old grandpa was like a dream to her.

After her separation from Ekwueme, she decided to heed his advice and told all the men who approached her for marriage that she no longer had a womb and as such, could never bear a child. They all took to their heels after her confession.

The situation was depressing, but she kept consoling herself. After all, she was the sole cause of her problems. One of the suitors blatantly told her that without a womb, she had become a man, and no man in the country would ever take his fellow man home to his mother.

One day, she visited her parents in the village and a young man came to their house to seek her hand in marriage. She was excited that her prayers had finally reached heaven, but all that excitement died when the young man mentioned that he needed a wife for his aged father, someone to take care of him and keep him company.

Initially, Ebony declined, but after two months of thinking, she decided it was best to settle for the only person who accepted her the way she was. That was how she got married to a sixty-year-old man. His children financed the traditional wedding and she moved in with him.

It was a sad and extremely tough experience for a young lady who spent most of her childhood dreaming about marrying a young and successful man. She could not count the number of times she laid on her bed as a kid and fantasized about the large wedding she was going to have and the kind of long, flowing dress she was going to wear. In the end, she had ended up holding a marriage ceremony that had less than twenty people in attendance.

Sometimes, she blamed herself for her past mistakes; other times, she blamed her friends for misleading her. Jealousy tore at her heart whenever she saw Ekwueme's wife, Juliet, on TV, speaking and enlightening people. It pained her because the lady was a lawyer and her former schoolmate. She remembered the lady from way back in university. She was among those who kept to themselves, studied their books, and went for inter-school competitions.

In just a few years, Juliet grew to be among the top young, successful lawyers in the country, and Ebony did not need a soothsayer to know that Ekwueme was partly responsible for the fast-paced success.

That could have been her. She wiped her tears, sighed, and tried to focus on getting ready for work. Despite how hard she worked in the past few years, her career was still at that point where she did not want it to be—almost at the bottom of the ladder.

Yes! She was a lawyer, but not the kind of lawyer she wanted to be. Growing up, she had wanted to study hard and help women and children who suffered various kinds of abuse. She had also hoped to have a foundation. But now, she could barely help herself, let alone help others. She still had a long way to go.

Minutes later, she was set for work. No matter how beautifully she dressed, or how well she made-up, she could still see her pain reflect in the floor-length mirror. She had become a sadist.

Ebony sighed and headed to the sitting room where she waved goodbye to her husband, before stepping out of the house, and into her car. She turned the key in the ignition and the engine came to life. Ebony was thankful because the previous day, the car had given her too many issues and she was worried it might not start.

Driving out of the compound, pictures of the kind of life she should be living flashed through her mind. She thought about the kind of cars Ekwueme had in his garage. The luxury car he bought for her as a wedding gift. The rickety car she drove was nothing compared to any of those cars, and it made her bitter with herself.

Ebony shrugged. Her husband was a retired public servant and getting his pension every month was a herculean task. Apart from that, the amount was nothing to write home about. Ebony practically took care of the bills and some other basic needs with her salary; that was not the kind of life she wanted.

"Well," Ebony murmured. "At least, I am alive, and I can afford three square meals in a day. I know a lot of people who did not get the kind of second chance I have now. I know some who died while having an abortion. I'm thankful for this second chance, even though I wish I could turn back the hands of time."

Streaks of early morning sunlight filled the private living room where Ekwueme was watching the news. The reporter was talking about a lady who had been declared missing a few weeks back and was later found in a hotel room, catching her fun with a man.

Ekwueme sighed. He had not forgotten Ebony and watching or hearing news of this sort made him wish ladies would stop selling themselves short for material gains. No, he did not regret letting Ebony go. It was the best decision he ever made; otherwise, how would he have had kids?

Ekwueme heard his smart and intelligent son, Ekene, singing loudly from the bathroom. He smiled at the thought that Ekene had left the door opened, as that is his way of enjoying his bath.

The boy is a joy to be with and Ekwueme knew he made the right decision about letting Ebony go. It is okay to adopt children if one is unable to procreate for whatever reason, but still, nothing beats having a child who shares one's physical features and intelligence. The joy around this was unexplainable.

One evening, during dinner, Ekene had asked his parents about his sister. He had wondered if his parents would buy him a sister or a brother.

Ekwueme and his lovely wife, Juliet, burst into laughter and promised to get him a playmate. It was a few weeks later that Juliet announced she was pregnant.

Initially, Ekene did not understand what was going on with his mother, or why her stomach seemed to be getting bigger every day. Ekwueme had to explain to him that his brother or sister was in there.

Ekene had been so excited. He told everyone who came visiting, as well as in his class, that his mother was about to give him a sister. However, after a scan to determine the sex of the child, it revealed twins—a boy and a girl. Ekwueme's joys knew no bounds and Ekene was over the moon with happiness.

Ejiofor and his parents congratulated him. He had pulled Ejiofor into a hug and thanked him for not keeping quiet over Ebony's past. For if he had, Ekwueme knew he would never have experienced the kind of joy and satisfaction he now had.

"Darling." His wife called from the doorway.

He looked up to see her looking beautiful in her nightie even with her protruding tummy. "Yes dear," he replied.

"It seems you're thinking again," she said.

"No, my love." He got to his feet. He switched off the TV and hurried over to meet her. "I'm only wondering why ladies out there are ruining their lives."

"Isn't that why we are enlightening them with our programs?"

"Yes," Ekwueme said. He took her hand and pulled her into his arms. "I'm happy you didn't ruin yourself for material things. I love you even more for that."

"I love you too dear," she said and wrapped her arms around his neck.

"What about me?" Ekene asked, running towards them with his wet body. He was coming from the bathroom and he never liked to miss a family hug.

Ekwueme and his wife laughed just before they lifted Ekene and hugged him. This is his family. This is his life. And this is what he is grateful for. His happiness is complete.

THE END

Author's Connect

You can reach him to have a chat on his books and movies via:

Website: www.chinazomgodwin.org

Facebook page: Chinazom Akobundu Godwin Books and Movies.

Instagram: chinazomakobundu

Twitter: @chinazomagu

Goodreads: Chinazom Akobundu Godwin

www.ingramcontent.com/pod-product-compliance
Lightning Source LLC
Chambersburg PA
CBHW071748150726
47998CB00005B/1846